JILL CHURCHILL

Bell, Book, and SCANDAL

AVON BOOKS
An Imprint of HarperCollinsPublishers

This is a work of fiction. Names, characters, places, and incidents are products of the author's imagination or are used fictitiously and are not to be construed as real. Any resemblance to actual events, locales, organizations, or persons, living or dead, is entirely coincidental.

AVON BOOKS
An Imprint of HarperCollins*Publishers*
10 East 53rd Street
New York, New York 10022-5299

Copyright © 2003 by The Janice Brooks Trust
Excerpt from *A Midsummer Night's Scream* copyright © 2004 by
The Janice Brooks Trust
ISBN: 0-06-009900-3
www.avonmystery.com

First Avon Books paperback printing: November 2004
First William Morrow hardcover printing: November 2003

Avon Trademark Reg. U.S. Pat. Off. and in Other Countries, Marca Registrada, Hecho en U.S.A.
HarperCollins® is a trademark of HarperCollins Publishers Inc.

Printed in the U.S.A.

10 9 8 7 6 5 4 3

*To Linda,
who gave me her watch.
Thanks!*

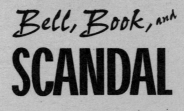

Bell, Book, and

SCANDAL

One

On a surprisingly mild day late in February, Jane sat out on her kitchen porch waiting for her next-door neighbor and best friend Shelley Nowack to come home. When Shelley's minivan turned into the Nowacks' driveway at about fifty miles per hour and screamed to a violent halt, Jane strolled over.

"Look what I got in today's mail," Jane said, shoving a brochure through the window of the minivan.

"Help me unload the groceries first. I have a car that's full of stuff that needs to go in the freezer," Shelley said, handing the brochure back without looking at it.

When the food was stashed away, they sat down at Shelley's kitchen table with the brochure. "A mystery conference right here in town. Cool. Are you going?"

"I want to," Jane said. "The book I'm writing isn't exactly a mystery, but I think all good novels are mysteries. At least, they need the elements of secrets that need to be unraveled, even if there isn't a crime. Will she give the guy a second chance to straighten up his act or won't she? Is there a chance he'll be named in his rich grandfather's will? Will the child recover?"

"I never thought about it that way. You're right," Shelley agreed. "And the conference is at that fabulous hotel near that new mall we've never been to."

"I wasn't planning to stay at the hotel," Jane said. "What's the point when it's so close to home?"

"There are two points, Jane. For one thing, you learn more from people if you're staying at the hotel at conferences. Other attendees usually have drinks at the bar at night, and that's when they reveal a lot more inside poop to friends and eavesdroppers.

"The other point," Shelley went on, "is that Paul has invested in this hotel and, as such, always has a suite on hold for his use. We could stay in it for free."

Jane had often wondered just how rich the Nowacks were, but hadn't asked and never would ask Shelley. Paul's investment must have been a substantial one, however, to rate a full-time suite. But the Nowacks lived almost as modestly as Jane did. Their house was the same size as Jane's. Their children went to the same public schools as Jane's did. Their wallpaper and carpets were only slightly more expensive than Jane's, in spite of the Nowacks' obviously being far more affluent. Shelley's husband owned an enormous chain of Greek fast-food restaurants.

"We? Would you really be interested in going with me?"

"Of course I would. I like knowing the inside poop about nearly any business. I don't think I'd go to an accountants' conference, but this one would be interesting." Looking over the brochure, she added, "I see by the schedule that there are usually two or even three tracks of speeches. You could go to one and I'd go to another and take notes for you. And late April is such a good time for a perk."

"I'll sign us both up," Jane said. "This will be really fun, I hope. Some of my favorite mystery writers are on the list of attendees. I'd love to meet them or least see and hear them in person."

"Let me jot the date down and tell Paul we need the suite that weekend if it's not already booked."

Three days later, Detective Mel VanDyne, Jane's longtime lover, dropped in after dinner and said, "I have a day off tomorrow. I've got more laundry than most armies accumulate in a week, the floors are dirty, and I'm buried in paperwork, most of which needs to be thrown away. Any way you could help me out?"

"Sure. Have you had dinner? There's leftover pot roast, gravy, and peas."

"Yes, please," he said pathetically. "All I had in the fridge was disgusting cottage cheese."

When he'd finished the leftovers, Jane said, "I have something interesting to tell you. . . ."

"Could it wait until tomorrow? I have to go home and get a start so you won't know how sloppy my apartment really is."

"It'll hold," Jane said.

When she arrived the next morning, the cottage cheese was gone. Most of the paperwork was gone and Mel had started the first load of laundry.

Jane took charge. "Get me the vacuum and the attachments."

"Attachments?"

"All those little gadgets that came with it. You start cleaning from the top down. There are cobwebs on the ceiling. There's a tube that sucks them up, and the same tube gets the dust off the blinds. Then you do the carpet. I'll start in the front bedroom. You finish throwing trash away and put your first load of washing in the dryer."

It took three hours before almost everything was clean. When Mel started making the bed, Jane realized he didn't even know the right way to tuck the top sheet in tightly at the bottom. "Mel, stop. Don't you know how to do a nurse's corner? Watch this and do the other corner like I do this one."

He was surprised. "My mother failed to teach me that. In fact, I don't know if she knew this. She always had a maid to do things like this."

Jane sat down on the bed when they were finished. "Don't you want to hear my good news?"

"I'd rather we made good use of this bed first."

Jane smiled, slipping off her shoes while saying "Me, too."

Later, while Mel went for carryout Chinese for their lunch, Jane took a look in the fridge and decided he'd have to deal with it himself. But she'd tell him all about the writers' conference over the egg drop soup.

As time went on, Jane and Shelley received updates on activities and speakers. Jane became more excited every time she perused one of the bulletins.

"You sound as if you know who these people are," Shelley said when Jane rhapsodized about one of the additional speakers—a woman named Taylor Kensington, who wrote superb romantic suspense.

"Not to say 'know' for real. I admit I've been subscribing to a publishing magazine ever since I started this novel. I've kept track of names and reputations."

"How so?"

"There are columns about big sales of manuscripts every week or two. The magazine sometimes knows, and tells, the amount of advance paid. They always name the publisher, the author, and the agent who sold the work. Lots are nonfiction, of course."

"Advance? You mean they give a writer money before the book even comes out in the bookstores?"

"Of course. Sometimes they give advances without anything but a concept that hasn't even been written yet."

"You're kidding! I've got a lot to learn about this, I guess."

"The terms of the contracts are often interesting, too. I wouldn't let you see one, however. Nor would I show it to an ordinary attorney for fear he or she would have a stroke."

"Why is that?"

"It's something they'd know nothing about and think was indentured servitude, I understand. That's why writers need agents who are used to the weirdness of publishing contracts. I hope there will be some seminars on contracts."

"You *will* show me the contract!" Shelley exclaimed.

"Not until I understand the rules well enough to explain them. Oh, Shelley, I may not ever see one at all, you know."

The conference was to start on Thursday, and the Monday before, Jane set out for the grocery store early with a long list of things her two remaining children living at home could eat while she was gone. Shelley was just coming home from some errands.

"You're not letting your mother-in-law take care of them this time?" Shelley asked.

"Thelma's got a conflict. She's going to her younger sister's house in Saratoga because the sister's husband is having very serious surgery and wants someone from the family with her in the waiting room. Besides, Katie and Todd are, I hate to admit, fairly responsible and should be able to take care of themselves."

"Right. But you're going to be calling them to check every five minutes, aren't you?"

Jane grabbed her purse and pulled out a cell phone. "I finally caved to technology," she said. "Isn't it darling? So very tiny."

"You didn't invite me to help you shop for it," Shelley complained. "I could have advised you."

"It was on sale for twenty-two dollars at the department store, and I'd seen another just like it for a hundred. How could I go wrong?"

"Twenty-two dollars!" Shelley almost screamed.

It was the same kind of cell phone Shelley had, and her reaction led Jane to suspect that Shelley had paid the full hundred for hers.

"I've made the kids memorize my number. They're to call me or leave a message every time they step foot out of the house."

"So much for you trusting them," Shelley said. "Did you buy them their own phones at this sale?"

"I regret to say I did. I figured they'd be a whole lot happier about the rules if they had their own phones. But I made sure that they can't call long distance on them, and when their free minutes run out, the phone doesn't work anymore until the next billing month starts."

"Good Lord! I didn't know you could do that! I've been afraid to let my kids have one for fear they'd run up huge bills. You remember when Denise stupidly called that psychic hot line and I got a bill for a hundred and seventy-five dollars?"

"Of course I remember. You tore through the phone company like Sherman through Atlanta to remove the charge. Anyway, I'll see how well the kids respond to the plan. And I'll hunt down any suspicious numbers when I receive the bills."

When Jane got into her ancient, disreputable old brown station wagon to go to the grocery store, it wouldn't start. She called Triple A and they sent a guy out right away.

"I'm sorry to say, Mrs. Jeffry, that this is beyond fixing unless you want to put thousands of dollars into it to get it running again. Where do you want it towed?"

Jane was crushed to have lost her old familiar wheels. On the other hand, it was a relief. She'd driven the big wallowing station wagon for too many years already. It embarrassed her to be seen in it. It had once been brown but had faded to a motley tan. The carpets were stained with Kool-Aid. There'd been a crack creeping across the windshield for the last several months. She'd known for a long time that she ought to rid herself of it while it still got her around.

"I certainly don't want to put money into the poor thing. And I have no idea where to tow it to," she said.

"May I make a suggestion?"

"Suggest away, please!"

"There are lots of charities that will take a car off your hands and you receive a tax break for the donation at the blue-book rate."

"It's certainly not worth the blue-book rate. And it doesn't even run. How would I deliver it to them even if they were foolish enough to want it?"

"They'd have it towed at their own expense," he said with a big grin.

"What charities?" she asked.

"I'm not sure. I'd guess the Salvation Army. But it's a guess. I had a customer who donated a dead clunker that was worse than this one to the Kidney Foundation. Got a computer? Look on the Internet for places that take them."

Two

Jane gave up on shopping and cruised the Internet. At noon, she heard a truck fall into the hole at the end of her driveway. She apologized to the driver of the tow truck.

"Never mind. I should have seen it and straddled it," he said. "Is this the car we're taking away?" He said this as if it were among the worst he'd hauled off for a long time.

"Poor old car," Jane said. "It's gotten me through becoming a widow, driving the car pools for a hundred years, hauling birdseed, groceries, and assorted misbehaving children. I'm afraid of what its fate will be. It's served me well."

The tow truck driver looked at her as if she were slightly mad.

Shelley, having heard the noise, came to her kitchen door in her jeans with an apron over a T-shirt. She looked out for a second, then disappeared.

By the time the station wagon was gone, Shelley had reappeared looking as if she'd just come from a beauty shop and stopped off at a very expensive dress shop.

"Why are you dressed so well?" Jane asked.

"Because this is what I wore last night to one of Paul's dinners for his employees. It was the closest thing at hand. Where's your car going? What's wrong with it now?"

"Nearly everything's wrong with it. I'm donating it to a charity."

"What? Somebody wants that car?"

Jane felt herself very nearly tearing up. "I think they're probably having it gutted and crushed. So they can sell the metal as scrap."

"Jane, it's a vehicle. Not a person."

"I know that, Shelley. I'm also having a new driveway put in and acquiring a new friend."

"A new friend?"

"A Jeep. You're too dressed up to go with me. Change your clothes to 'business casual' as they're calling it in the ads on television. We have an appointment to buy the car this afternoon at two-thirty. Would you drive me? I have no wheels of my own."

"A Jeep? Good idea. One of those really big ones, right?"

"No. It's a new, smaller one called a Liberty."

"How did you find out about it?" Shelley asked as Jane trailed along while Shelley headed for her own kitchen door.

"I looked it up on the Internet. Called Mike after he got out of his nine o'clock class at college and asked him a few questions about what I needed for choices. Boys in their twenties always know this stuff and love showing off about how much they know. Then I called several dealerships to find out if they had what I wanted. Fortunately, the closest one to our neighborhood did."

"Start us a pot of coffee while I change, please," Shelley said.

The coffee was poured and Jane had found some stale vanilla wafers to snack on.

"What color are you choosing?" Shelley asked when she came back in black silk trousers, low-heeled gray patent heels, and a white linen blouse with a gorgeous scarf draped to perfection.

"Red. But only if I like it when I see it. Maybe taupe. They have both options with what I want on the lot."

"What did Mike say?"

"After he screamed 'Whoopee!' you mean?" Jane replied. "He told me to pick a certain kind of brakes. I've got it all marked out on the sheet I printed out. Heated leather seats. A sunroof. Fancy tires. A CD player and tape player both. The best that they've got at the dealership."

"Jane, you amaze me!"

"Why?"

"Because you've always been so stingy with yourself. First that big television set in your bedroom, now an expensive new car. I can hardly believe it. Good for you."

"For one thing, it isn't as expensive as you're

imagining. Not even close to the cost of a Humvee, which I almost considered until I found out the price. I would look so good driving a Humvee.

"Secondly," Jane went on, "it would have cost several thousand to fix up the old station wagon, and it wouldn't add anything to its trade-in value. I donated because I can take the book value off my taxes, and that's a lot more than it would be worth if I turned it in. And I'd be deeply embarrassed to let a car dealer even see it."

"How did you learn all about this?"

"I have my sources," Jane said smugly.

"You're turning into me, you know."

"That's a good thing," Jane said. "But I'll never spend what you do on your wardrobe, I can promise that," she added with a smile. She glanced at her watch. "It's only twelve-fifteen. My appointment to buy the car isn't until two-thirty. I have to go to the bank first to buy a certified check. What else can we do to kill time?"

"We can go look at your list and check the site on the Internet for color choices. Wouldn't you rather have a nice bright green or maybe a white one? Or even that cobalt blue color you like?"

"White would glare in the sun and always look dirtier than it really is. They don't have a bright green. Only a dark green."

"Go for the red then. Taupe is only good for clothing. But you'll have to see it in person to decide. I sort of liked that shiny blue one. But colors on the Internet aren't all that reliable."

"As long as I wouldn't have to wait for it, I might buy the blue," Jane said. "I don't want to waste a month or six weeks to special order and drive a rental. Let's go have lunch before we go to the bank. Those soggy wafers aren't enough to fortify me for such a big decision."

Later, fortified by a sandwich and caffeine, Jane had her check in her purse, and when they arrived at the car dealership a full twenty-five minutes early, Jane began dragging Shelley around the entire lot looking for her choices. She was reading the sales slip on the window of a metallic blue car when Shelley said, "I see your car, I think. Come this way."

And there, in its full glory, was the car Jane wanted. "It doesn't look dark red," Shelley said, "It has too much purple in the red."

"It's called garnet," Jane said. "Not dark red. And I don't think it's the least purple. It must just be these weird pole lights that make it look odd. It's a shame it's such an overcast day. I still want to look at the taupe. It's the color of the interior of this one."

"Can't we just go inside and see if your salesman is twiddling his thumbs waiting for us to show up?"

"What a good idea."

"You do know, don't you, Jane, that I'm not

good with car salesmen? I always want to tell them off for treating me like 'the little woman' who doesn't know a car from a dishwasher."

"Then don't speak at all and let me sort him out," Jane said. "I Am Woman."

As much as she wanted to dislike the salesman, Shelley couldn't. There wasn't a hint of patronizing. He was even impressed by Jane's computer printout of her shopping on the Internet and the fact that she had brought it along to show him what she wanted. When he went to fetch some paperwork, Shelley admitted he was treating them well.

"He doesn't know I have a son who told me exactly what to choose. He thinks I know all about these brakes I've selected."

Both of them got impatient with how long it was taking, however. There was a guy Jane had to talk to about an expensive extended warranty, and she was ready for this as well, thanks to her son. A third man wanted to sell her a package of expensive extra things, like a sealer to prevent rust and a lot of other stuff she hadn't been warned about. The total for the extras came to nearly a thousand dollars.

"I think not," Jane said firmly.

"But if you buy the whole package, it's only three hundred dollars," he said.

"I'll think about it and let you know while they're bringing my car to the door," Jane said.

"That's insane!" Shelley hissed when they were

out of his hearing range. "Each part of the deal cost nearly the three hundred. Does he think we're idiots who can't add it up?"

"He's young and stupid and we're probably older than his mother," Jane said. "I might spring for the three hundred bucks. But I'm not doing it until I've driven the car for a while."

In the end, the salesman made Jane drive the car with him in the passenger seat and Shelley in the backseat. He was pointing out where all the features were, which disconcerted Jane, although she thought he didn't know he was frazzling her.

When he said, "This handle turns the windshield wipers on," she glanced down very briefly at a stick that said "Pull." She tried pulling out the end knob. He said, "No, that means pull it toward you."

"Oh, of course."

There was a low growl from the backseat, which Jane ignored.

When the test drive was over, the forms all filled out, the check approved, the temporary license plate in place, and everybody had shaken hands in a distinctly "manly" way, Shelley said, "I wish we'd taken a cab so I could ride home with you."

"Have you ever seen a cab just cruising our street? And would you have paid him to sit around when we stoked up on sandwiches and coffee? And then run us to the bank?"

"I guess you're right."

"We'll take a nice long drive when we've stopped by home," Jane said. "By the way, I'm never going to smoke in this car or let anyone else do so. I've made a vow that it's not going to lose its new car smell ever."

"I've never seen you smoke in the station wagon."

"That's because I only smoke three cigarettes a day, and sometimes only one or none if I'm really busy and forget. But I have on occasion opened the window while I was waiting on carpool kids and stunk it up."

She went on, "Where shall we take our drive after we drop your car off?"

Shelley said, "Shopping. Anywhere *except* the grocery store."

Three

Jane really wanted to go to the courthouse to have her temporary license plate changed over to a real official plate for her new car. But going there was never a fun thing to do. Her memory, so long ago when she bought the station wagon, was a bad one of surly crowds, disobedient children running wild in the corridors, and having to return two times because the clerk said she didn't have something she needed in the way of paperwork.

"How long had you had the station wagon?" Shelley asked.

"I can't remember. I had to turn over the title to the man who took it away, and I forgot to look at how old it was. I think I had it for at least twelve years."

"I'll bet it was longer than that."

"You might be right. Where shall we go?"

Jane wanted to do something fun and so did Shelley. Shelley was already calling on her cell phone before they'd gone a block. "May I speak to the manager, please?"

After a moment or two of silence, she introduced herself and said, "Oh, John. I'm so glad you're the one on duty. Is the Nowack suite open now? I want to show it to my friend who's staying with me in it for a couple of days." Another silence. "Oh, good! We're on our way."

"What a good idea," Jane said, turning left at the next intersection.

She was uneasy about parking in the hotel lot next to someone who might bang his door into her brand-new car. She parked as far away as she could, where there weren't other vehicles.

Shelley knew why she was doing this, and for once kept silent.

They got out and Jane fumbled for a moment with the gadget they'd given her to lock the doors. She was surprised the car made a pitiful little beep and the lights flashed briefly when she pressed the lock key. "That's neat, isn't it? It's telling me it's worked. I wonder if it'll do it when I unlock it as well."

"Jane, stop playing with your car and come inside," Shelley ordered impatiently.

It was a very long walk and Jane kept looking back at her car, thinking the thing she liked best about it was the big round headlights. So retro. So 1930s. So pretty. She could have driven it around Gosford Park and felt right at home. But she'd yet to drive in the dark and would have to read the manual to figure out how to turn on the lights.

"Isn't it a gorgeous lobby?" Shelley exclaimed

when they walked into the hotel, as if she'd designed it herself. "Jane, pay attention. Forget the Jeep for a bit."

It was a great lobby. It was enormous, but cozy at the same time. In spite of vast expanses of marble flooring, covered with what one could mistake for real Oriental rugs, it had lots of comfy seating areas where you could have a private discussion with friends without anybody overhearing you—unless you were yelling.

"This is really luxurious. Look at these floors. Some of it has fossils, doesn't it?"

"I think your imagination is in overdrive," Shelley said, dragging her along to the check-in desk, which looked as if it were a huge piece of furniture from a very old castle, except that it was too clean and shiny.

"Mrs. Nowack," the manager said. "That was fast."

"We're in my friend's new car. This is Mrs. Jeffry, my roommate when we come to the mystery conference."

The manager knew which side his bread was buttered on and studied Jane for a moment, clearly noting her and memorizing her name.

"I'll escort you ladies upstairs."

"No need," Shelley said. "I've been here often enough to find it myself. Just loan me a key."

She led Jane to the most magnificent elevator she'd ever seen. Almost the size of a large room, it was mirrored with dark green glass with a touch of gold, with light green marble in narrow stripes between the mirrors. It had a lush carpet, and there was even a little plush bench you could sit on.

"I could park my car in this elevator," Jane said.

"Not today, please," Shelley said, pushing the button for the top floor. The elevator ascended in absolute silence.

They stepped out into a very wide hallway. This floor was inlaid with marble as well, this time an off-white with brown speckles. The same quality of runners ran down the middle as the ones in the lobby. It was well lit with lovely lily-like sconces in pinky-mauve glass that were set next to each door.

They headed left to the far end and Shelley inserted the plastic credit-card-like key. "Voilà!" she said, pushing Jane ahead of her.

Jane gasped. She thought the room was the most beautiful place she'd ever seen. Colorful without being gaudy. They'd come first into an enormous parlor with a big dining room table at one end with eight Windsor shield-back chairs. There was a matching server bureau with a fabulous floral arrangement of real flowers. The air in the room was lightly scented by the roses.

The other end of the parlor was furnished with comfy-looking chair-and-sofa combinations. Three groups, with big coffee tables so a lot of people could sit down and visit and eat or drink without having to balance their plates on their laps.

"Explore," Shelley said. The room was on a corner and light filtered through the windows clear around two sides through sheers. There were what looked like well-lined silk floor-to-ceiling curtains that could be drawn for privacy, even though no building near it was taller.

Off to the right was a small, exquisite kitchen separated by a serving bar. The stainless steel cabinet doors had a swirly pattern that echoed the lily look of the lighting fixtures in the hall. Jane opened one door and found a vast array of fine glassware. There was a little refrigerator under the counter and next to it a separate ice machine humming along quietly.

"Come on, Jane. See the rest of it," Shelley said, leading the way to the right to a master bedroom. It was as luxurious as the parlor. There was a king-sized bed and a mob of throw pillows; a desk near the window that looked like a genuine antique, but probably wasn't; gorgeous table and floor lamps with the swirly steel pattern and light pink shades.

"Wait till you see the bathrooms," Shelley said smugly. "Paul and I chose our own fittings at the Merchandise Mart."

Jane cringed slightly at the memory of Shelley having dragged her through the Merchandise Mart. Jane had been wearing unsuitable shoes, and carrying a big purse that kept banging into things and becoming progressively heavier for no good reason.

The bathroom was, in fact, magnificent. Huge. Light green marble floors, lots of elegant bath rugs that didn't slip around. "The floor is heated," Shelly said smugly.

Jane leaned down to feel it and it was warm. There were also a pair of the fluffiest bathrobes Jane had ever seen. There were both a bath and a shower.

"That's the one we saw at the Merchandise Mart, remember?" Shelley said. "The shower that's computerized to be instantly the temperature you want. Six showerheads, programmed to hit as hard or softly as you want."

"What are the two little rooms that open off at the far end?" Jane asked.

"The toilet in one and a bidet in the other."

There were plush towels hung on pewter racks and extras folded on glass shelves set high enough not to bang your head on them. There was also a standing heated towel-and-bathrobe rack.

"Shelley, I have to say this is the most beautiful bathroom I've ever been in. You really did a great job."

"Your bathroom off the other bedroom is exactly like it, except the color scheme is different."

"Let's go look."

Shelley's bath was all in shades of green and

blue. Jane's was apricot and muted lemony colors. Jane liked hers better. It seemed warmer and more inviting.

They came back into the parlor and sat down on one of the sofas. "There's only one problem with this," Shelley admitted.

"I sure don't see what it is," Jane said, glancing around.

"Pull any of the sheer curtains away," Shelley said.

"Good Lord. It overlooks the top of the mall. All those ugly refrigeration devices and air vents all over the roof," Jane said.

"The view from all the windows is awful all the way around," Shelley admitted. "But then, you never really need to look outside."

"I do. I can see my car from here. I'll have to park it in the same place when we come back."

"Admit it, Jane. You'd forgotten about your car for a few minutes."

"Not entirely."

Shelley sat back comfortably on the sofa and said, "You'll be meeting a lot of people at the conference. Feel free to bring anyone you like up here."

"Should I? I don't think so."

"Why not?" Shelley asked.

"Because they'd think I'm a rich dilettante just trying to write as a silly hobby."

"Just tell them your roommate is the rich dilettante who doesn't aspire to write anything but shopping lists. I'll even pretend it's true if it's necessary. The writing part, in fact, is true."

"Okay," Jane agreed. "As fabulous as this suite is, I need to go home. I want to take a copy of my manuscript to the conference, just in case somebody is willing to look at it."

"You've really finished it?"

"I think I have. Having a real deadline to meet helped. There are a few little dinky things I've marked to fix. And I was educated so long ago that I'm not certain about commas in series."

"The rules don't change," Shelley said.

"But they do, Shelley. Grammar isn't static. And most of what I learned in the many schools I attended as a kid in Europe involved British grammar and spelling. They do things differently."

"Like how?"

"For one thing, they use a single quote for dialogue, and a double one inside it for a word that's emphasized. Americans do it the opposite way."

"You know the weirdest things," Shelley mused. She rose and gathered up her purse. "Have you got everything you brought along? You don't really need to keep those car keys in your hand so tightly that your knuckles are white."

"I've got to hang on to them until I can put the duplicates away somewhere safe," Jane said, going once more to look out the window to enjoy a bird's-eye view of the new car.

As they descended in the elegant elevator, Jane said, "I think I'm going to need to tie something gaudy to the luggage rack on top. I don't think I'd have recognized it in a parking lot if it hadn't been sitting way off by itself."

Four

The conference registration was to begin at one-thirty Thursday afternoon. It had been Shelley's advice that Jane call the hotel at ten in the morning and ask if the suite was ready.

"You need to be the first one there. Meeting and greeting, you know," Shelley said. "There are always people who come early. People who have family in town to visit, or business to conduct privately, maybe shopping and such."

Having been assured that the suite was available, Jane gathered up her manuscript and took one long last look at it for errors. She found only two and ran out new pages. She packed it in a box and put it in a canvas bag. She also had a copy of the first three chapters and the outline of the rest of the book in case she came across an agent or editor who was interested. She'd read somewhere that this was a necessity at a writers' conference.

She'd even shopped a bit in the interval between seeing the suite earlier and returning to it. Three casual skirts, four blouses with coordinated lightweight sweaters. She also had black trousers and a sparkly black top for the banquet night. She'd even dug out a few pieces of jewelry that she seldom wore. A sapphire and diamond ring her parents had given her for her twenty-first birthday. A cheap but good-looking silver linked necklace that made her neck itch if she wore it for too long.

It was more than she needed, but she didn't want to miss a moment running home if she spilled coffee on herself.

Jane arrived at the hotel at ten and went to the suite. She'd thought about hauling the manuscript to the lobby and studying it one more time. But that would look too needy.

Instead, she took along a copy of the latest Felicity Roane book with her. She positioned herself close to the front desk, so she could glance up from time to time and see if she recognized any of her favorite mystery authors. There had been photographs of them in the last brochure she'd received.

She saw a man who had to be Zac Zebra arrive wearing black trousers and a black sweater thrown over a shiny white shirt, open at the neck too far. He had black-and-white-striped hair. She knew he was one of the speakers. Did they have their rooms paid for? she wondered. He took out a credit card, but that meant nothing. Even when you had a free room, as she did, hotels wanted a credit card for incidentals like food, drinks, and dry cleaning.

She went back to reading her book, glancing up from time to time.

A woman who might be Felicity Roane herself checked in about ten minutes later. Jane glanced at the formal photo on the back of the book. If this was Ms. Roane, she was a lot more casual than the picture. Her hair wasn't up. She had a wind-blown ponytail with a scarf around it. She was in jeans and a baggy lightweight gray sweater.

Jane hoped this was the author she liked so much, and liked, too, that she seemed less daunt-ing than the photo. It was all Jane could manage to stay seated. She wanted to run over to the front desk, book in hand for autographing. But Ms. Roane might have had a long trip and wouldn't want to be fawned over while waiting for her room assignment.

She went on reading, so caught up in the story, in spite of the fact that she'd already read it when it had come out in hardback, that she probably missed several other famous attendees. When she finally looked up the next time, Shelley was checking in. Jane put a bookmark in the book, stuffed it in her purse, and approached her just as the bellhop was taking up her suitcases.

Fishing in her pocket, Shelley pulled out a five-dollar bill and tipped him before turning to Jane. "Have you spotted anyone yet?"

"Zac Zebra," Jane said. "Nobody could mistake him. And a woman I think was Felicity Roane. But I'm not positive it was she."

"Where are you sitting?" Shelley asked.

"Right over here. Don't you want to go up and unpack?"

"I'd rather gawk with you for a while."

While they watched the front desk, chatting about what fun the conference was going to be, a rather heavy, terribly overdressed young woman came in. She and the man with her were wearing cowboy hats and flashy western clothing and lots of turquoise jewelry.

"Probably country-western singers performing somewhere in Chicago, don't you think?" Shelley asked. "Nobody dresses that way for no reason."

"Maybe. Or maybe they're just rubes come to the Big City for the first time."

"I'm going to ask who they are," Shelley said. "Watch my purse," she added as she strode off.

"Excuse me," a voice said from in back of Jane.

Jane, startled, stood up and turned. "You're Ms. Felicity Roane, aren't you? I was hoping to meet you."

"I noticed you as I came into the hotel," Ms. Roane said, sitting down in the third chair in the grouping. "I'm always looking at people on planes reading, hoping to see them reading one of my books. The only time I did, I made a fool of myself. The woman was right across the aisle and I said it was so nice to see her reading that book. She just looked at me blankly and said that it was the only one in the airport with a nice cover. She clearly didn't recognize me," she said with a laugh. "I told her I wrote the book she was reading and she said, 'Of course you did.' I didn't know if she meant it or thought I was crazy.

"But I spotted you reading my most recent paperback," she went on, "and thought I'd give it another try. Would you like it autographed?"

"Oh, yes please, Ms. Roane," Jane said while she fished the book back out of her purse.

"Please, don't call me Ms. Roane," she said with a smile. "These mystery conferences are really casual. Everybody calls me Felicity. And old friends call me by my real name. Freddy for Fredricka. Feel free to call me anything that starts with F, except the F-word, and I answer." She took the book and got a pen out of her bag. "And you are . . . ?"

"Jane Jeffry. And the woman approaching us is my next-door neighbor Shelley Nowack."

"Jane Jeffry is a good name. You're sure you didn't make it up? Are you a writer or reader or both?"

"Both," Jane admitted. "So far unpublished though. I came here to learn tips on how to market my book."

Shelley had returned and introductions followed.

"That's what everybody who wants to crack the shell should do," Felicity went on. "And what about you, Shelley?"

"I have no writing aspirations, though I read a lot," Shelley said. "I'm just along to help out Jane.

I'm planning to go to different lectures to take notes because she can't be in two or three places at one time."

"Shelley isn't quite telling the truth," Jane said with a laugh. "She writes the best letters of complaint you can imagine."

"A skill I wish I had," Felicity said. "Where are you ladies from?" she said, signing the book with a flourish of green ink.

"Only a few blocks away," Shelley said. "Would you sign another one for me later?"

"I'd be delighted. Have you had breakfast yet? I'm starving. Will you join me? Just give me ten minutes to change out of my airplane garb and fix my hair."

Jane was thrilled but refrained from gushing. "We'd like that."

When Felicity was out of earshot, Shelley said, "This is astonishing. John at the front desk said those cowboy people checked in as part of this conference. And there was another odd thing I overheard. That Zac person who's been lurking near the desk went up to the woman and young man checking in. He gave a paperback book to her, saying, 'Sophie, you *must* read this.' "

"That's sort of strange," Jane said, still preoccupied with how very nice Felicity Roane had turned out to be.

Felicity met them at the door of the hotel restaurant shortly. Now she looked a lot more like the photo on the back of her books.

When they'd ordered, Felicity said, "Have you seen any of the others arrive? I'm a bit early. I always like to get rid of the airplane hair and rest up my white knuckles before I go into author mode."

"I saw Zac Zebra," Jane said. "There's no mistaking him." She studied Felicity as she spoke. The author had put her hair up in a twist at the back and was wearing freshly pressed tan slacks and a pink blouse. A lovely soft scarf draped over her shoulder was held in place with a pretty gold pin.

"Zac must go to every mystery conference in the country," Felicity said. "He's an unforgivable show-off with that crazy hair. He claims to have written several books under a pseudonym, but I don't believe that. For one thing, nobody's really named Zac Zebra, are they?"

"I hope not," Shelley put in. "Do you already know all the other guest speakers? Do you do this a lot?"

"I know most of them. But not, thank goodness, the E-Pubbed Wonder."

"Who is that?"

"I've forgotten her name. Deliberately, I fear. She posted a book on the Internet. She's quoted as saying her wonderful husband sold his pickup truck to fund the publication of it."

"People pay for being published?" Shelley said with horror.

"Some do," Felicity said. "I've never heard of

any of them actually making back the money though, until this hick turned up. She had the nerve to send it to Sophie Smith."

"Who's Sophie Smith?" Shelley asked.

Jane knew the answer but let Felicity reply.

"The toughest old editor in the business. She's called other names I won't repeat because they're obscene. Most of us have had her at one point or another. To our sorrow. She has a reputation for buying up anybody she can get her hands on and just splatting their books against a wall to see who sticks. Once every couple of years, she fires upward of two dozen who haven't flogged their book sufficiently to live up to her sales expectations. I was one of those. Not only once, but *twice*." She admitted this with a wry smile.

Jane was liking Felicity more and more as she went on. She had the same self-deprecating sense of humor that showed in her books. She could criticize others with abandon, but also make fun of her own mistakes just as could her heroines.

"What did this Sophie think of the e-pubbed book?" Shelley asked.

"She loved it and so did that assistant of hers, Corwin. Rumor is, she paid a fortune for it. It's apparently told in two alternating viewpoints, chapter by chapter. Sophie must have thought that was a truly original thing to do. I don't think Sophie has ever read anything that wasn't by one of her own writers or she'd have known better."

"Is it still on the Internet?" Jane asked.

Felicity shrugged. "I don't know. I never looked for it. Other writers I know thought it was awful. Pretentious. A sort of conflicting quest for both characters. Lots of misspelled words. And those who read clear through it said the ending stunk. The two viewpoint characters had never even heard about each other until they met in the last chapter, and it was apparently a very boring meeting. Of course, this all might be just sour grapes. All of this gossip came from the struggling mid-list writers like me who are beating their fingers to a pulp to keep up."

"Mid-list?" Jane said. "But you've had a lot of bestsellers."

Felicity laughed. "If you claw your way onto the bottom of the one hundred and fifty books on the *USA Today* list, your publisher can call you a bestseller. But I have a good many readers who genuinely like the books and keep on buying them. And most of them are still in print, so I consider myself very lucky."

"Aren't there other authors who have self-published their work, which eventually led them into real publishing?" Jane asked. "I've heard of a few, but don't remember who they were."

"Neither do I," Felicity said. "But I do recall that a few of them became really big names and made tons of money."

Five

Over their last cup of coffee, Shelley asked Felicity about the other guest speakers. Glancing down at the brochure she'd received in the mail, she asked, "What about this man Chester Griffith? He's a bookseller, it says."

"That's a very modest bio. He's a lot more than a bookseller," Felicity said. "He's the antidote to Zac Zebra, for one thing. Zac is a macho pig who only gives good reviews to tough-guy books. On the rare occasions Zac critiques a book by a woman, he's vicious. His favorite phrase is 'powder puff mysteries.' And he claims to read ten or twelve books a day. Which is ridiculous. If you've read the book he's reviewing, you can tell that he only reads the back-cover copy and imagines what the book is about. He mixes up characters with each other and he's notorious for giving away the endings, with men and women both."

She sighed. "I'm sorry I'm ranting. To answer your question, Chester Griffith is an intelligent gentleman though he doesn't mince words. He

makes no bones about saying that women writers
are superior at their craft. He's practically memorized all the Golden Age female mystery writers'
output. He's the world's expert on Agatha Christie, Margery Allingham, Ngaio Marsh, and several less-well-known women. He's researched their
lives as well. He's a good speaker.

"He also likes what he calls 'the Modern
Golden Age' writers. Emma Lathem, Dorothy
Simpson, Gwendolyn Butler, and Ruth Rendell's
Wexford novels as well. With the exception of
Christie's Miss Marple, all of these women wrote
about male protagonists with a sensibility that's
missing from tough-guy books."

"I'm going to like this man," Jane said. "The
names you've mentioned are nearly all of my favorites. I've reread many of them."

"But Zac Zebra says all these women's male
protagonists are wimps, if not downright homo-
sexual."

"You're kidding?" Jane asked with disgust.

"I've heard him say it to whole groups of fans,
many of whom walk out on his speeches," Felicity said.

"Why do the people who plan the conferences
agree to let him take the podium?" Shelley asked.

"Most of them, I suspect, think he spices up a
conference," Felicity said. "I myself think he's a
pollutant of the usual goodwill between readers
and writers."

"What about Taylor Kensington?" Shelley

asked, again consulting her brochure. "Should one of us go to her talk? It says she writes two different series and one of them has an historical setting."

"Taylor Kensington is a delightful woman," Felicity said. "Very funny, very low-key. One of my best friends in the business. She's a trooper who has helped a lot of aspiring writers. I like her suspects, her settings, her plots, which are so well researched, but . . ."

"But what?" Jane asked. She'd recently read one of Kensington's novels and hadn't liked the ending.

"She writes heroines who, at the end, stupidly go out in the middle of the night all alone to investigate suspects. In every one of her books, the woman is nearly killed for being suddenly so dumb," Felicity explained.

Jane said, "I've only read one of her books and that's exactly what happened at the end. The character seemed so smart all the way through, and then went out to a deserted construction site at four in the morning to meet a stranger who tried to kill her. I wanted to slap her silly."

"I'll jot her name down to avoid reading, nice as she might be," Shelley said, scribbling a note on her brochure.

"Who is this Miss Mystery?" Jane said, still perusing the most recent mailing. "I'd never heard of her and she's the only one without a picture."

"Oh dear. I didn't know she was coming," Felicity said with slight alarm. "I should have read the last bulletin they sent. She has an Internet site where she critiques women's fiction. She slaughters the work of newbies and e-pubs. She also puts her saber through the guts of the most successful, genuinely bestselling women writers. Struggling mid-list authors are her cup of tea. I should be grateful, I suppose, being among that group. But I'm not. She's a lot like Zac in that she merely skims the book and mostly misses the whole point of the work. I think it's a power thing. I've actually seen a couple of paperback originals who cite her in the blurbs."

"Blurbs?" Shelley queried.

"You know, those 'I love So-and-So's characters. They're so vibrant.' Signed by a well-known author."

"Blurbs. I'll have to remember that. I'm a sucker for them," Shelley admitted. "If someone I recognize and like to read says something nice on the cover, I'll buy the book."

"That's the point of blurbs," Felicity said. "And it's usually a good guide to book shopping. Avoid the book if it's blurbed by Miss Mystery though."

"Why isn't there a picture of her?" Shelley persisted.

"Because she comes to conferences under her own name and chums up with authors to acquire the dirt on other authors. Nobody knows who she really is."

"That's sneaky," Jane said. "So why is she even listed in the brochure?"

"To warn the authors that she's around, I suppose," Felicity replied.

After the waiter had interrupted to give them their bill, Shelley said, "I'd guess somebody recognizes her."

"Why?" Felicity asked.

"Because if I were to tell some stranger some deep secret of Jane's—which I'd never do, needless to say—and later saw her report it on her website, I'd remember who I'd spilled the beans to."

Felicity stared at Shelley with astonishment. "Of course!" She made a head-slapping motion. "You're right. Some people must know who they blabbed to and about. But they don't dare admit it."

"Rest assured," Jane said, "neither of us is Miss Mystery."

Felicity grinned. "You promise?"

"Girl Scout's honor," Jane said, raising her hand.

Their discussion was suddenly cut short when a couple came through the door of the restaurant. It was the country-western pair Jane and Shelley had seen entering the hotel. The woman looked around and shouted a sort of yodeling greeting of "Yippee! I reckon y'all are the mystery writers," she said, raising her hefty arms as if embracing the whole room. Her turquoise and silver jewelry jangled.

Heads turned with annoyance.

"I'm Vernetta Strausmann, and this is my ever
lovin' hubby, Gaylord. Pleased to meetcha, y'all."

She glanced around the room and spotted Fe
licity and screeched, "*Omigod!* It's Felicity Roane
You're my favorite author!"

Dragging along Gaylord, who looked both
proud and embarrassed, she galloped over to
their table. She all but jerked the chair out from
under Jane.

"Here, honey, let me grab this chair. You se
yourself down over in that one. I gotta hug my fa
vorite writing gal."

Jane grabbed the bottom of her chair and held
her ground. Felicity had her arms extended
palms out, to stave off the hug. She was blushing
at being singled out so outrageously in public.

"I'm sorry, but I'm having a chat with friends
Maybe we could meet later," Felicity said coldly.

"Pretty wimpy friends, it looks like," Vernetta
said, her expression turning mean, her eyes going
piggy, and her already strident voice becoming
even louder.

"They're *my* friends and you aren't," Felicity
said firmly.

"Who'da thought you were such a bitch!" Vernetta screamed, looking around the restaurant to
make sure everyone was listening. "You're just
jealous of me because I'm gonna make a lot more
money than you'll ever see. C'mon, Gaylord."

She stomped out. Gaylord leaned toward the

table and said, "Miss Roane, I'm surely sorry 'bout this. She don't always mean what she says. It's what she says is 'artistic privilege.' "

Felicity was obviously having trouble suppressing tears of rage.

"What a terrible woman," she said in a shaking voice.

Six

Somebody in the restaurant clapped a couple of times, and most of the other patrons joined in. "You go, girl!" one woman said, raising a fist to Felicity and grinning.

Felicity relaxed a little and waved back. "I need another jolt of coffee," she said under her breath.

"Why don't you come up to our room for it," Shelley asked. "There's anything there you'd like to drink."

"Let me take care of the bill first," Felicity said.

"No, you won't. Not after you told us so many interesting things," Jane said. "We'll take care of yours."

"Nope," Felicity insisted. "My cost is tax-deductible."

She hailed a waiter to pick up the bill, and during the slight delay, several of the other diners came over and asked who that awful woman was. Or who Felicity was. Several who weren't even attending the conference had heard of her and asked if her books were for sale and could they catch her later to have them signed.

As Felicity scrawled her real name on the credit card slip and put the card back in her purse, she said to Jane and Shelley, "Who'd have thought that scene would have paid off so well?"

They strolled through the lobby and looked over the registration booth, which was just opening up for business. They each were given a canvas bag full of goodies, including a complete booklet giving the times and rooms where each session would be held and extensive bios of the speakers; free books by writers who were attending; pens with authors' web sites; bookmarks with lists of the author's books; and even a tiny pink-and-white box of peppermints from one writer. Jane and Shelley studied the booklet. It was much more complete than any of the materials they had received earlier.

"Jane!" Shelley exclaimed, "turn to page four. It's a picture of Mel."

"Good grief. He didn't tell me he was a speaker. How sneaky," Jane said.

"Who is Mel?" Felicity asked.

"Jane's honey," Shelley said.

"Damned good-looking man," Felicity said.

Jane flipped to a page at the back and said, "Wow! There are agents and editors here that you can see and talk to privately for fifteen minutes," Jane said. "I had no idea. Which would be a good one, Felicity?"

"Let's take it up with us and look it over," Felicity responded.

Felicity was frankly astonished at the suite Jane and Shelley were staying in. Shelley had to explain, with enormous modesty, that her husband had invested in the hotel and that part of the deal was having the suite be available to his family or friends when it wasn't otherwise booked.

Jane was impatient but tried not to show it. She wanted desperately to return to the registration booth before all the editors and agents were booked up. As they'd waited for the elevator, quite a few attendees had already lined up.

Felicity appeared to sense her tension and the reason for it. "Let me look at that. Oh, they're all baby editors and agents."

"Babies?"

"New ones with names like Tiffany and Bambi. But that's okay," Felicity said, "if they're babies in a good agency or publishing house. There are normally only a few heads of houses or agencies at small conferences like this." She pulled out her green-ink book-signing pen and checked three. Two agents and one editor.

"These are with good companies. And they're eager to come back to work with something to show for being sent here at their employers' expense."

"I don't see Sophie Smith on this list. Isn't she a really important editor?" Jane asked.

"Yes, but she leaves things like this to her underlings. Downtrodden people like that poor Corwin she drags around with her and abuses in public. You don't want to be with her anyway."

"What would you both like to drink?" Shelley asked them.

"I'll have a soft drink, something brown. Coke or Royal Crown if you have any," Felicity said. "And Jane needs to run back downstairs and make her appointments before the slots all fill."

"Thanks," Jane said. "I think we're twins separated at birth. RC is my favorite, too."

"Are you prepared for these interviews?" Felicity asked.

"I have the whole manuscript with me, but I didn't think anybody would want to weigh down their luggage with it."

"Do you have the first couple of chapters and an outline with you?"

"Yes, I do," Jane said.

"Good for you, girl!" Felicity lifted a fist as the woman in the restaurant had done. "You've done your homework. Now scat. Oh, let me write my room number down. Call me when you know who you sign up with."

Jane returned to the suite forty-five minutes later. Shelley was sitting in one of the chairs with her bare feet up on a coffee table, reading a book. "Did you find who you wanted?"

"Amazingly, I did. Sometime between now and

tomorrow morning I have to run home and make copies. Just on the faint hope that all three will want to see the chapters and outlines."

"There's a copy shop in the mall just across the parking lot," Shelley told her. "Spring for their prices and don't waste your time going home."

"Where did you find that book? It's Felicity's latest. I already had a copy you could have read."

"Jane, where is your head?" Shelley exclaimed. "Authors come to these things to sell books. There's a room just to the west side of the registration desk where there are four booksellers. I wouldn't dream of borrowing your book and cutting down on what she earns on this. And besides, I want it autographed to me."

Jane slapped her head. "Do you have any more RCs? Somebody stepped on my foot in line and I need to put it up for a few minutes."

"Not the foot you broke?"

"No, the other one," she said, taking off her shoe and rubbing her little toe as Shelley brought her a drink.

Shelley said, "I've been thinking about that Zac person. Felicity said he'd written a couple of books. I'll bet that's why he was forcing one on Sophie Smith. Wanting to get back in the game."

"You could be right. He'd probably make a better living writing his own books than reviewing others. And if he continued to do both . . ."

Now that she had Jane's agreement to her theory, Shelley said, "Let's pick out what to wear at

the dessert bar tonight, then we can go have your
copies done, and you can have part of the afternoon to mingle."

"I'm not a very good mingler," Jane admitted.

"Everybody has these tags with their names on
them. Just approach anyone standing alone and
introduce yourself. Easy as pie."

"First, I must call Felicity while I'm still shoe-
less and tell her I lucked into the appointments I
wanted." But Felicity wasn't in her room and Jane
left a message.

"See, Jane? She's out mingling," Shelley said
smugly.

Jane pointedly ignored this and glanced again at
the schedule. "I want to go hear what Sophie Smith
says this afternoon at the opening ceremony."

Going to the copy shop wasn't exciting but it
was better than trying to make lifelong friends
with strangers. Jane took her outline and the
chapters and had three copies made. She
bought three simple buff-colored folders to put
them in, forgoing the copy shop's more attractive folders—floral, neon transparent, and a
pink she liked. She knew, however, that making
something "cute" was the sign of an amateur.
She chose the fourth folder in bright orange for
her own copy. She simply couldn't resist.

When she returned to the hotel, she parked
closer to the copy center than to the hotel itself,
then trudged clear across the increasingly hot

pavement and went up to the suite to leave the copies. She was still hot, so she had another soft drink. She also called the front desk to ask if Mel VanDyne had checked in yet. The clerk said he was booked to arrive the next day. Knowing full well she was dawdling, she finally broke down and went to the lobby.

Jane mingled to the best of her ability. A few of the seemingly lonely attendees were simply waiting for the rest of their friends to arrive. Jane introduced herself anyway, and said how much she was looking forward to this conference. "I've never been to one of these. Have you?" she asked the first woman she accosted.

"Oh, I go to all of them. I'm an autographed-book junkie. Oh, there's Susan. Nice to meet you, Joyce."

"Jane," Jane said to herself as the woman disappeared.

A couple of the solitary figures she tried to mingle with seemed to want to latch on to her for dear life. She was nice to them, but eventually did the same thing the first woman had done to her. Pretending to see a lifelong friend. But Jane said the women's names right.

She met two other rather aggressive unpublished authors who hoped Jane was an editor or agent. This was quickly sorted out. They hadn't realized until then that the name tags were color-coded in order to differentiate among fans, writers, editors, agents, and booksellers.

She gave up trolling the lobby and went to the booksellers' room. This was, naturally, a much better experience. People who love books love promoting their favorites to other people who love books.

Jane struck up several cheerful conversations with shoppers from the conference who insisted she buy several authors she'd never heard of before.

When she forced herself to stop running up her credit card, she had a bag of books she could hardly manage to carry back to the room by herself.

"Good Lord!" Shelley exclaimed when Jane staggered back to the suite. "Have you bought out all four booksellers in one swoop?"

"Almost. But look at what neat things I've bought," Jane said, sliding the pile out of her canvas bag and onto the coffee table. As she lined them up and fondled all of them, trying to decide what order she'd read them in, she said, "I'm going to have to buy more bookshelves. But I'll tell you this, Shelley, the best mingling is that room."

"You're not going back in there, are you? You'll break the bank."

"Maybe not right away," Jane said.

"You sound guilty."

"Three of the four bookstores are from the Chicago area. I asked for their business cards so I can look at everything they stock, not just the selection they brought along. I also bought a really nice computer program to keep track of what you've read, how much you liked it, and whether there are more books by the same author. And a really cool book-holder gadget. I bought one for you, too."

Shelley just shook her head and said, "Do you want to go down for lunch before the opening ceremony?"

"I'd rather eat room service so I can look over all these books."

Shelley tossed her the room service menu. "Read this first. I'll order."

Seven

Todd and Katie were out of school that day due to a "professional development workshop" the teaching staff had to attend. Jane pried herself away from the book collection for long enough to call the kids at home. Katie's new cell phone was busy, which made Jane frown. Who was her daughter already using her precious minutes on? She called Todd's number and he picked right up.

"Hey, Mom! You're my first call. This is so cool."

"It is, isn't it? Where is Katie?"

"Right here, trying to call you at the hotel," he said. "Wanna talk to her?"

"Sure. Hi, Katie. Hang up your phone," Jane said to Todd.

"Is the conference what you expected?" Katie asked. "Are you having fun?"

"Lots of fun. I have three appointments with two agents and an editor tomorrow."

"You're going to sell your book, Mom. I just know you are."

"I'm not counting on it but I've already learned a lot about the business. Hold on. Room service is at the door," Jane said.

"I've never had room service," Katie said with a slight whine, when her mother came back to the phone.

"Yes, you have, Katie. Remember when we took that trip to Colorado? We called room service there. What are you doing tonight?"

"Jenny's coming over. We're making spinach omelettes with lots of cheese."

"I'll check back with both of you after the dessert welcome party tonight," Jane said.

Jane had dithered over choosing what to eat, so Shelley had chosen cheeseburgers, french fries, and salad for both of them. They both sat at the big table in the suite. They used the nifty book holders Jane had bought in the book room, reading and chatting while they ate.

"I never knew these things existed," Shelley said. "Thanks."

"I didn't either. Aren't they great?" Jane said. "When I read while I'm eating at home, I usually just prop the book open with a knife and have to keep moving it. Sometimes I forget I've used it and smear up a page with mayonnaise or catsup."

"I'm going to save my salad as a late-night snack, so I have room for desserts."

"Plural?" Jane said.

"Of course. I've been to things like this before. They cut lots of different desserts into really tiny pieces and let you try out a lot of them. You know, I came here not only to snoop and enjoy this suite, but also to help you out. I'm having more fun than I expected. Wasn't all the inside gossip your friend Felicity told us neat stuff to know?"

"She's such a nice woman, isn't she?" Jane said. "I'm amazed she took such pains to fill us in on the people here. I'm only sorry that awful woman Vernetta was so rude to her."

"I suspect a lot of other people here will feel that way before this conference ends," Shelley speculated. "I have my laptop along. Later on, we must take a look at her book on the web. As illiterately as she speaks, I can't imagine it being any good."

"To be fair, she might have a good story in her head in spite of it," Jane said, doubtfully.

"You don't need to be fair to a person like that, Jane. She's scum."

"I guess you're right. And I'm sure the publisher will clean up her grammar and spelling for her if they paid big bucks for it. I wonder if Vernetta will even notice."

"Probably not. Jane, I can't finish my fries. Do you want them?"

"No, thanks. Let's just put this away in the little fridge. It's only half an hour until the opening remarks. Plenty of time to wash the catsup off our faces."

*   *   *

At the start of the opening session, Sophie Smith took the podium. She stood silently for a moment, waiting for the conversations to stop.

"She's sort of swaying," Jane observed.

"Yes," Shelley said. "Nerves?"

"I wouldn't think so. She must have done this dozens of times, and everybody says she's a tough cookie."

Sophie began to speak, paused a moment, and disappeared behind the podium.

The young man, Corwin, who'd been checking in at the desk with her that morning, and a couple of the staff of the conference who sat at the head table, ran over. Conversations broke out, all wondering what had happened. Had she been standing on some sort of box and fallen off? "No, she's a tall woman, she wouldn't need a box," somebody piped up.

"Let's get out of here," Jane said.

As they headed for the door, they heard someone come to the podium and say, "Ms. Smith has been taken slightly ill. There's no need to be worried. She's being well taken care of. She's left her written introduction to our speaker. Everybody sit down and I'll read it on her behalf. . . ."

Jane and Shelley closed the door behind them.

"I think she was taken a bit more than 'slightly' ill," Shelley said. "Did you see the look on her toady Corwin's face as he bent over her? He looked horrified."

"I hope she's not dead," Jane said. "It would cast an awful pall over the rest of the conference. They might even cancel the rest of it. Oh dear, I shouldn't have said that. It sounds so selfish."

"I think if she is dead, it might be the highlight of the conference," Shelley said. "She seems to be heartily disliked by everyone but Vernetta."

Other attendees were slipping out as well, either having heard how boring the speaker was, or out of dismay at the scene they'd just witnessed.

Jane and Shelley took over a couple of chairs and a table in the hotel lobby. "I could ask John, the hotel manager, if he knows what happened. If he's on duty this shift," Shelley said.

"I don't think he'd tell you even if he knew."

"Probably not. But I'll give it a try."

Shelley returned a few minutes later. John was in a meeting and couldn't be disturbed, she reported.

The lobby was filling up with writers and fans, all speculating about what had happened. Some said, sounding knowledgeable, "She's had a heart attack."

Others stuck with the theory of her just fainting. Or falling off whatever she might have been standing on.

One suggested that the wiring was bad and as she touched the microphone she'd been electrocuted. This was hooted down. "The woman who ended up reading the speaker's introduction touched it, too, and nothing happened to her," someone said.

"This is driving me mad," Jane said. "Nobody knows what they're talking about. Let's go somewhere else. We have half an hour before the next seminars."

Shelley picked up her purse. "There are some nice shops in a tunnel under the hotel. Let's go shopping for therapy."

"I'd rather go to the book room again," Jane said.

"No, you wouldn't. It would be full of other attendees saying the same things. Come with me. Last time I was in the tunnel shops, I saw a lapel pin I thought you'd like, and now that I see you in this sweater, I know it would be perfect. Let's see if it's still there."

The last seminars of the day both seemed exceedingly boring, so Shelley and Jane went upstairs and finished the salads they'd put in the tiny fridge. Jane checked in with Todd and Katie again on their new cell phones. Katie said the omelettes were almost ready and she couldn't talk right now. Apparently this overrode the thrill of receiving a call on her new phone.

Shelley and Jane arrived five minutes after the dessert party started. It was already crowded. Shelley had been right. The desserts were all about one and a half inches square, set in little paper baskets. Jane picked up a plate and selected only three. She didn't want to look greedy. And she could always dispose of the plate and go back, pretending it was her first trip.

Both Jane and Shelley were keeping a wary eye out for Vernetta and Gaylord Strausmann. They didn't want to be taken unawares again.

"I'd have thought a big hefty woman like that would be the first through the line," Shelley commented as she forked up a sliver of cherry cobbler.

"I'd have thought so, too," Jane said around her mouthful of a bread pudding square liberally iced with sugar and brandy. "Oh, there's Felicity surrounded by fans, while we're nobodies who have our own table so we can stuff ourselves without being noticed."

At that moment Vernetta and Gaylord entered the room. As she did in the restaurant, she shouted, "Howdy, y'all. I'm Vernetta Strausmann and this is my hubby, Gaylord."

The pair had abandoned their country-western look and gone for pure June and Ward Cleaver. Vernetta was in a patterned shirtwaist with the buttons straining at the bodice. A little fifties hat, high heels, and even white gloves, a bit grubby at the fingertips. Gaylord was in a gray suit and wore a fedora and shiny black shoes. The outfit would have looked more authentic if the trousers hadn't been a bit short and his black-and-red-striped socks hadn't been showing.

"Do they think this is a costume party or Halloween?" Shelley said. "Where did they find that stuff? At a secondhand store?"

Most of the people in the room were staring at the couple, but nobody approached them. Vernetta looked over at the crowd surrounding Felicity and glowered. Gaylord took her arm in a firm grip and whispered something to her. She nodded and smiled hungrily at the other party-goers.

"Gather round, y'all. Lookee-loo at the plans for our mansion."

She took over the largest table, forcing two women who were eating there to find other seats, and unfurled a couple of large blueprints. Gaylord found some canned drinks to hold down the corners. "Come on, y'all. Don't be shy," Vernetta bellowed.

A few obedient people eased their way toward the table.

"See? Here's the second floor," Vernetta said. "Ten bedrooms. The biggest for Gaylord and I, and one for each of the three kids. And six more for guests."

"Gaylord and *me*," Shelley muttered, turning her back on the scene Vernetta was making. "Just imagine the absolutely spine-chilling horror of being their guests!"

Jane scooted her chair so she wouldn't have to watch, though they were forced to listen.

"This here room on the ground floor is a ballroom," Vernetta went on. "But we're gettin' lots of tables and chairs for when I set up giving writing lessons."

Jane was hard-pressed not to put her face in her plate and weep.

"Finish your desserts and we'll replace our plates and round up some of the stragglers to sit at our table and mingle," Shelley said. "Maybe we can talk loudly enough to drown her out."

Corwin, Sophie Smith's assistant, came into the dessert room, picked up two little pieces of bread pudding, and sat down at a corner table, first putting the other three chairs against the table as if he was saving them for someone else.

Vernetta dragged Gaylord across the room and grabbed two chairs, setting them upright and settling in. "How swell of you to have kept chairs for Gaylord and I."

Gaylord grabbed her arm again and whispered. Vernetta lowered her voice to his command, leaning forward and resting her enormous breasts on her crossed arms on the table while chatting to Corwin, asking him pointed questions about how Sophie was doing. In a few moments Corwin rose and leaned over Vernetta and said something to her.

Vernetta and Gaylord rose and left the table. The young man tilted the chairs back toward the table to finish his desserts. "Toodle-loo, Corwin!" Vernetta said in a little girl voice as they drifted away.

"I wonder what he told them?" Shelley said. "They don't look angry about being dismissed."

Jane said, "He probably said they could talk

with her editor later in private, or some such tactful remark. I'm amazed it sunk into the Strausmanns' brains—such as they are."

The two minglers Shelley and Jane had hijacked were trying to convince Shelley to buy a book by their favorite author. He apparently wrote very blunt and hard-boiled police novels, a type of literature Shelley didn't like.

Their new tablemates finally rose and left, giving one last order that Shelley buy the book they liked. As they departed, Jane looked around the room and realized the crowd was thinning a little. She and Shelley went for their third course of desserts, but there wasn't anything left that they hadn't already tried. They went back to the booksellers' room. Unfortunately, it was shut down for the night, so they had no choice but to either keep mingling in the lobby or go upstairs to the suite.

"I'm mingled out," Jane said. "And I want to have a good night's sleep so I don't look half dead in the morning. My first appointment is at nine o'clock."

Eight

Sophie Smith had endured what were probably the three worst hours of her life. She'd had her stomach pumped because the first resident to see her thought she'd been poisoned. The full-fledged doctor who saw her next put it down to a virus and took blood samples. Between and after these ministrations, Sophie had spent two and a half disgusting hours in the hospital room bathroom. She was afraid of leaving the tiny tiled room for fear of disgracing herself.

By seven o'clock in the evening, she was finally able to crawl into the extremely uncomfortable bed.

She rang the hotel and gave her own room number. "Corwin?"

"Yes?" her assistant said. "Who's calling?"

"It's Sophie, you ass."

"Sorry. You don't sound like yourself."

"Of course I don't, Corwin. I've been through a wringer."

"I've called the hospital three times and nobody

would tell me anything about your condition," Corwin complained.

"They're insisting on keeping me in here overnight for observation. No point, really. I'm feeling better already."

"Do they know what was wrong?"

"They have half a dozen theories. But I'm tempted to find where they've hidden my clothes and make a break for it. Whatever it was, I'm nearly over it."

"Sophie, you must stay there. What if you have a relapse of whatever it was?"

She'd actually considered this and said, as if she were graciously taking his advice, "I guess I might as well stay until morning, though I fear these horrible sheets will take a layer of skin off me. Meanwhile, Corwin, bring me that book bag, would you? And my purse. I need to show these people my health insurance card. Both are in the bottom of the closet. Make sure that thing Zac Zebra handed me is still in the book bag."

"Let me look right now," Corwin said.

He came back in a moment. "Are we talking about the paperback book?"

"Yes."

"It isn't in the book bag. Could you have put it somewhere else?"

Sophie, for all her bravado, knew she still wasn't quite up to par mentally.

"I may have taken it out of the book bag. I don't remember doing so. Perhaps I set it aside somewhere. Take a good look around the suite and bring the bag and my purse," she said, knowing she was whining.

"If you don't find it," she went on, "ask Zac Zebra to find another copy. I simply can't imagine being stuck here without something to read, and since I don't know where my clothes are, I can't even walk down to the gift shop. My hospital gown gaps in the back. Come over as soon as you can. And bring along a small bottle of Merlot. Carefully hidden, of course."

Early Friday morning, while Jane was drying her hair, she was astonished when a phone rang in the bathroom. She hadn't even noticed it was there.

"Hello?"

"Mom," Mike said, "I've been told that you, Katie, and Todd all have cell phones. Why don't I have one?"

Jane laughed. "Because you were in college instead of home the day I went haywire and bought them."

"Are you still haywire?"

"Yes, but for different reasons. I'm at this mystery conference, as you obviously know because you have the telephone number to my room. I have appointments with two agents and one editor today."

"I know. Katie told me. Congratulations. But about the cell phone . . . ?"

"You'll be out for summer vacation soon. I'll buy you one then. Okay?"

"Okay. Good luck, Mom. I have to be in class in five minutes. Gotta go. There's a test today and I have the crib sheet up my sleeve. Just *kidding*, Mom."

A moment later, Shelley turned up in Jane's room. "I heard the phone. There's nothing wrong, is there?"

"No. Just Mike wanting to know why the whole family except him received cell phones."

Shelley laughed. "What a good grapevine your kids have. Do you have time for breakfast before your first interview?"

Jane looked at her watch. "Nope. How about we meet after the interview? It's only twenty minutes from now and only fifteen minutes long."

"I'll meet you at the registration booth then. Do you have everything you need for the interview?"

Jane rolled her eyes. "Yes, Mommy."

When Jane arrived in the interview area early, she peeked in the door. Three tables had been set up in the room where the dessert party had been held. Each had two people sitting on opposite sides and a placard with the name of the editor or agent. She was early, so she sat down on a chair in the hallway, waiting with the two other eager, nervous interviewees. They exchanged smiles all around, but didn't speak.

A few minutes later, the door opened and two

women and one man walked out. One woman was smiling. The other two people looked disappointed.

Jane and the other two women she'd waited with rose and entered the room. Jane went to the desk with a card saying "Gretta Green." This was the first agent she had an interview with.

Jane leaned across the table and shook the woman's hand. "I'm Jane Jeffry, and I'm pleased to meet you, Ms. Green." She handed over the folder with the first three chapters and the outline.

The agent pulled out the papers, set aside the chapters, and went to the outline first.

"Oh, it's an historical novel, isn't it?"

"Yes, but it has a mystery element, too."

"But it's historical," Ms. Green said with a frown. "I hate to be the bearer of bad news, but historicals are dead and gone. Nobody's doing them anymore."

Jane didn't know quite what to say to this, but pulled herself together and managed, "But I've read a lot of historical mysteries that have been recently published."

"Yes, maybe so. But mystery is the main thrust of the books, not the historical element. And the outline suggests that's almost all historical. I'm sorry. It's not something our agency does. Good luck. It's been nice meeting you. Take my business card in case you decide to rewrite it as a pure mystery."

She handed back the folder, gave Jane her business card, and smiled dismissal.

There was nothing for Jane to do but thank her and get the hell out of the room.

She glanced at her watch once she was outside in the hall. Her fifteen-minute interview hadn't lasted quite four minutes.

Shelley could tell it hadn't gone well when she spotted Jane moping at the registration area.

"Struck out?" she asked sympathetically.

"I was in there less than four minutes, Shelley. She said it's too much of an historical novel and not enough of a mystery. Odd how fast someone can devastate someone's hopes."

"How could she tell that fast?"

"She skimmed the outline and made a prune face."

"She's an ignorant child, Jane. I took a look at her through a crack in the door. She can't be more than seventeen. Pay no attention. You still have two interviews to go. And you need to put this one out of your mind. When is the next one?"

"At the break at three this afternoon. This little girl who tossed me out had the nerve to give me her business card and said I could contact her if I rewrote the book."

"No! That sure takes a lot of gall. She obviously isn't the agent you'd want, no matter what. The other agent is a baby agent, too, isn't she?"

"Yes, and she's named Tiffany. She's probably fifteen years old," Jane said.

"Buck up, Jane. Breakfast will give you the energy. The first session starts in an hour and we need to coordinate who goes to which seminar. You go to your first choice, of course. And tell me your second choice and I'll go to it and take notes like mad."

Shelley's brisk orders helped Jane over her disappointment. But only a little bit.

The restaurant was crowded. Fortunately, most of the guests were finishing up breakfast and Shelley and Jane were served in a relatively short time. In the brief spell between the ordering and the arrival of the food, they'd worked out the schedule for the morning seminars.

Jane would attend "Time and Again," about historical mysteries, and Shelley would take notes on "Brightening Up Your Submission."

They wolfed down their food and headed to separate meeting rooms. Unfortunately, Gretta Green was one of the speakers and cited Jane's book proposal, though not by specific name, as a perfect example of what her agency didn't want to handle. She was the first speaker and Jane wanted to bolt to the suite and have a good cry. But she stuck it out.

The second speaker was a grown-up editor. At least thirty-five years old. And as politely as she could, she told the group that Gretta was wrong.

"Readers of both sexes like a strong sense of different times and circumstances. It's a wider audience than most agents realize." She listed by name several of her publishing house's best-sellers that were as much history as mystery.

Gretta just smiled condescendingly through this part of the introduction as if she knew better than the seasoned editor. Jane was glad she'd stayed.

The third speaker was an historical writer of some renown for yet another publisher, and she backed up what the editor before her had said.

"I've received more fan mail for the first two books in my historical series than I earned from all ten of my first books, which had a contemporary setting," she said.

She also went on to explain that she'd cut her publishing teeth on category romances, as many other writers had, and she and they had come to mysteries or thrillers with a lot of experience in writing and found it a wonderful change from the restrictions of short romances. Many of these former romance writers, including herself, had done historical romances and knew their way around research.

Although Jane wasn't among this group, she found the information very interesting and enlightening. Maybe Gretta, the baby agent, had spoken a shred of truth. Jane told herself that when she went home in a couple of days she'd look over her manuscript one more time.

The author went on to give some even better advice. "Lots of research into the period is vital, of course. You have to like doing this. More important, though, don't put in everything you know. It makes it a history text, not a novel. My own rule of thumb is when I find some fact that makes me slap my head and say 'I never knew *that*,' it's what should go into the book. If I didn't know it before, probably many readers don't know it either and will be pleased to learn it."

Jane wrote this down in her notebook and underlined it. She remembered making a house plan and leaving out bathrooms. She had had to do a lot of research to find out what sort of "facilities" her imaginary house would have had in the time period and may have gone a bit overboard describing them in her manuscript.

The introductory remarks having been made, the speakers then called for questions from the audience. Jane was surprised to learn that many of the aspiring writers in attendance were quite ignorant about the world of publishing. Some of them asked downright silly questions, like would submitting their work on pretty colored paper make them noticed.

The panel overwhelmingly agreed this wasn't to be done.

Another asked if she should copyright the work herself before submitting so nobody could steal her work. This struck Jane as absurdly arrogant.

This also met with a negative reply from all three of the speakers. "If the work is good enough, it will be purchased, not stolen. And the publisher will see to having it copyrighted," the grown-up editor said.

Most of the rest of the questions were either trivial or about technical things, like whether to use single or multiple viewpoint.

Jane came out of the session revived and cheerful. For one thing, she'd realized she still had a lot to learn. More important, she already knew more than most of the other aspiring writers.

Shelley's session had ended slightly earlier than Jane's, and she was waiting outside the door of the meeting room with a big batch of notes to hand on. "It's a good thing I'm a fast note taker."

Jane glanced at the notes and said, "You sure are. But some of this you're going to have to translate for me. What does 'D and A' mean?"

"Delivery and Acceptance of the finished manuscript, of course. Was your session good? You look like yourself again instead of half dead."

"It was wonderful. I can't wait to tell you about it." Jane pulled out the brochure to double-check. "I've changed my mind. I'm going to the viewpoint meeting. I think I still have a lot to learn about that. You can still go to the one about 'The Grammar Demon,' whatever that means."

Shelley gave Jane a quick hug. "I'm so glad you came and let me come along. This is so good for you, and even I'm enjoying it a lot. See you at the luncheon."

Nine

Jane discovered that the seminar called "Everything about Viewpoint" was more interesting than she'd expected and was glad she'd picked it out to attend.

There were only two speakers, both successful writers.

The first speaker was a very pleasant woman in her mid-forties, who, like one of the speakers in the previous seminar, had started in romance before turning to mystery. Orla Witherspoon said, "I was used to third person, single viewpoint. If you're not familiar with this term, it means the whole story is told from one person's point of view. But in the third person, as in 'Susan looked around in awe at the scenery and found it beautiful.' "

People in the group either nodded or scribbled in their notebooks.

Jane smiled. The reactions told a lot about who were the "girls" and who were the "women."

Ms. Witherspoon went on, "When I started the

first book of my first mystery series, I continued this just because I was in the habit of doing so. But it became onerous. I was ending up with all sorts of convoluted statements like 'Susan looked at Joe and suspected that he wasn't telling the truth.' "

"Or," she went on, " 'Andrianna was apparently a very shy woman.' Having a whole book full of 'suspecteds' and 'apparentlys' and 'possiblys' and 'almost-certainlys' and 'it-seemed-as-ifs' is tedious and boring to both the writer and the reader. And it puts too much emphasis, in my opinion, on one character. The richness of fiction, to my mind, is learning how characters feel in their own minds.

"I was fortunate to discover this," she continued, "before I turned in the manuscript. It's always best to start as you mean to go on. I decided I, and the reader, would both like the book better if I did multiple viewpoints. I had to do a monster of a rewrite, but it was a much better book.

"However, I only go into two, or occasionally three, viewpoints in any given scene. If you have a crowd of people interacting, you don't want to know what every single one of them is thinking."

She went on, "Now, I warn you, this is only *my* opinion, strong as it is. Our other esteemed author, Daisy Ellis, does third-person single viewpoint and I love her books. She's much better at it than I was," she added with a big smile as she introduced the other speaker and sat down.

Daisy Ellis, probably a good ten years older than Orla, stood at the microphone and was just as gracious. "Orla and I have been good friends and fans of each other's work for about ten years, and we've learned to agree to disagree."

"I'll say!" Ms. Witherspoon agreed heartily.

Ms. Ellis spoke just as confidently as Ms. Witherspoon had. "My purpose is to make the reader identify with the sleuth. Really be in his or her mind. Know what she or he knows, suspects, or concludes. I think it makes for a stronger story line as the sleuth investigates, finds dead ends, identifies and broods over what may or may not be genuine clues to the mystery."

She went on, "A lot of this depends on what the writer is comfortable doing. Be sure to realize that neither approach is right or wrong. Orla's books are, frankly, deeper than mine. But mine, I believe and hope, are enjoyed by just as many contented readers. And it's what I'm comfortable writing. And I know from experimenting with one book, I don't do multiple viewpoint half as well as she does. Now let's hear what all of you think about this, or want to ask about."

The group had lots of good questions for both speakers. Slightly more of them were directed at Ms. Witherspoon, about the technicalities of being in a number of characters' minds. Who should dominate the story? How could you go into the mind of the perpetrator without giving away the solution? Or didn't you ever go into the perp's viewpoint? If so, wasn't that a sure sign that he or she was the murderer? Ms. Witherspoon fielded these questions with explanations.

When Ms. Ellis was questioned about the main character speculating on the other characters' traits without the problems Ms. Witherspoon had listed, she said, "I let the characters speak and act for themselves. The reader usually draws the same conclusion as the sleuth does. I have no problem with writing, for example, 'Porky replied shyly,' or 'Violet became angry.'

"That's what my first-person sleuth thinks," she went on. "Sometimes the sleuth later finds out it was the wrong impression. And so does the reader."

Everyone had so many questions that when the allotted time ran out, they straggled out of the room still asking the speakers and each other questions.

Jane thought it had been a very enjoyable and well-prepared argument between friends and philosophies. She was glad she'd attended. And worried that Shelley's seminar must have been boring compared to her choice.

Jane was right. Shelley said dramatically, "You have no idea how deadly that was. I'm so glad I was at the back of the room and could slip out."

"You didn't learn anything interesting?"

"No, not really. Just what you said. The rules of punctuation change with the times, and various publishing houses have their own rule books they follow. Some are out of date, some don't care as long as the writer is consistent to his or her own rules, some don't care at all. They handed out lists of style sheets and recommended asking your publisher in advance which grammar and punctuation book you should follow. Imagine someone who's never published yet, asking a question like that."

"I'm so sorry I stuck you with that," Jane said. "The one I went to was wonderful. By the way, I haven't seen anything of the cowgirl Wonder Woman all morning, have you?"

"I heard that Vernetta crashed one of the other seminars in the middle of the second speech and made a fool of herself," Shelley said. "So she's still kicking. Didn't Felicity say Sophie Smith never appeared at conferences very much unless she was the single speaker?"

"Yes, I think she did. What did Vernetta do, specifically?"

Shelley said, "I didn't care to hang around the people who were ranting against her long enough to find out. But she and her hubby were in new costumes."

"Oh, what now?"

"Hawaiian," Shelley said. "I saw them when they left the room where it was held."

"Grass skirt?" Jane asked.

"In silver tinsel instead of grass. With paper flowers around her neck. Gaylord in the ugliest floral shirt I've ever seen, shorts, and sandals, and

beat-up straw hats on both. Gaylord's legs are
white and skinny. They looked like raw chicken
legs. Vernetta's legs are dimpled lard."

"You're making this up, right?"

"I am *not*."

"Are we going to the luncheon?" Jane asked.
"I've heard rumors that the guest speaker is
boring."

"We've paid for it in our fee. We might as well
try it out. If it's good, we can eat it. If not, we can
find our own lunch. I wonder if Felicity is free?"

"She's probably required to show up and mingle with fans," Shelley said. "It's in her best interest even if she doesn't have to attend. We can sit
near the door and slip out before the speech. Pretending we're taking a potty break, if anyone at
our table asks."

The luncheon, as it turned out, was extremely
tasty and came to the table hot. "We should have
guessed it would be good," Jane said, "considering how terrific those desserts were last night. We
are sticking around for dessert this time, too,
aren't we?"

"Of course we are. We can bolt it down and run
away."

"And go shopping," Jane said.

Ten

Shelley found the pin she'd seen. It was no longer in the shop window, but Shelley insisted they must have at least one more somewhere. When she offered, quite firmly, to help the assistant manager find it in storage at the back of the shop, suddenly the young woman remembered where it was kept.

Jane agreed it was exactly what she needed. And the price was much less than she'd feared. Shelley spotted a few new pieces of jewelry in the shop and made Jane try on a ring that had the same pretty paste stone as the pin. Jane didn't normally wear any rings at all for fear they'd either be impossible to squeeze back over her knuckle or be big enough to fall off unnoticed.

But Shelley said it fit perfectly and would do neither. Jane plunked down her credit card. When Shelley was so sure of something, there was no point in arguing. Shelley would just come back and buy it for Jane as a gift.

Jane put the pin on her sweater, the ring on her

finger, and said, "We're going to be late for the one-thirty session. Let's go."

Unfortunately, none of the one-thirty sessions especially interested either of them, so out of loyalty they went to the one where Felicity Roane was a panelist.

Even Felicity looked bored by the topic, which was "Planning Your Own Future in Publishing."

One of the baby agents went on and on about how your agent could map out a plan to follow.

"And what if the agent decides to have a baby and is off work for the first two years of its life?" Felicity asked. "Things like this happen. Editors become agents to make more money. Editors move to other publishing houses at the speed of light. Agents move to new agencies and writers get stuck with their assistant, who hasn't ever read one of your books and doesn't want to."

She went on, "As an author, the only thing you can control in this business is the quality of your work. And your reputation as a professional—producing manuscripts on time, making sure there are as few errors as possible. Not behaving as if you were their only author."

"Oh dear, Ms. Roane, these things you've cited that go wrong at the publishing end don't happen that often," the baby agent said with a giggle.

"How long since you graduated from college, my dear?" Felicity asked with a smile, but with fire in her eyes.

"Only two years. Vassar," the baby agent answered proudly. "But I've learned a lot about the business since then."

"I've been publishing my work for twenty-one years," Felicity said. "Bear with me. I really do know just a *little* bit more about this than you do."

The moderator jumped in and changed the subject and directed an extremely innocuous question about customary contract terms to another of the panelists.

"Poor Felicity," Jane said to Shelley under her breath. "She's running out of patience with fools, and I don't blame her."

The rest of the session wound down without any other problems but not much information either. Shelley and Jane went up to the speakers' table when the session was over. Everyone but Felicity had already fled. Felicity had taken out her contacts and was dumping everything in her purse hunting for her glasses.

She glanced up at them, smiling. "I made a bit of an ass of myself. But I was right and that little girl wasn't."

"Everybody knew that," Jane said.

"At least I'm done," Felicity said with a sigh. "I have no more obligations. Don't you have an appointment pretty soon with that editor I suggested?" she asked Jane.

"At three," Jane said.

"I think you'll like her. She's a grown-up. That's a pretty pin on your sweater."

Jane went back up to the suite to retrieve her second copy of the first three chapters and the outline. Shelley came along. "What session do you want me to attend while you're busy?" Shelley asked.

"I don't see anything very interesting," Jane said, glancing at the brochure. "Why don't you just veg out?"

"No, I'm going to go back to that shop and buy another of those pins so that we can give it to Felicity."

"What makes you think there is another one?"

"Didn't you notice? The girl came out with two boxes. I'm going to snag the other one while I can. Felicity's been very nice and candid with us. And she needs a pick-me-up."

Jane chose the copy she meant for the very good editor Felicity had recommended. This copy had something extra.

Months before, when Jane had broken down and bought a new computer, she had also bought a house plan program. The majority of her plot took place in an old rambling mansion perched on a cliff and backed by a village where a few of the scenes played out. She'd used the program to make a floor plan of the house and a map of the village as well. It was what had really inspired her to make a serious attempt to finish the book. This packet included copies of both the floor plan and the village map.

The editor was reading a book when Jane came into the meeting room a few minutes early.

The editor looked up and said, "You must be Mrs. Jeffry." She stood up, leaned over the table, and shook Jane's hand. "I'm Melody Johnson."

"I know you are," Jane said with a smile. "Felicity Roane told me to be sure and see you. She thinks very highly of you."

Melody Johnson appeared to be well into her forties, beautifully groomed, and casually, but stylishly, dressed. She wasn't what Jane thought of as "New Yorkish." She could have been a neighbor of Jane's.

"And I of her," Ms. Johnson said. "Let me see what you're clutching in your hand with a death grip."

Jane laughed and handed over the folder.

Ms. Johnson flipped through the pages and said, "A very nice presentation, Mrs. Jeffry."

"Please call me Jane. It scares me when people call me Mrs. Jeffry except if they're salespeople."

"And I'm Melody," the editor replied as she continued to examine the manuscript. "Oh, house plans! And the layout of a village! I love books with relevant illustrations. These are very good. Would you be so kind as to bring us both soft drinks while I skim the outline?"

Jane was over the moon. She could hardly make her legs work right as she headed for the snack table. She picked up two plastic cups of ice-cold Coke and dawdled, watching as Melody Johnson read the outline.

When Melody looked up, Jane crossed the room and set the drinks on the table.

"Have you finished this book?" Melody asked. "Or is this what you plan to do?"

"I've finished it," Jane said. "At least I thought I had before I came to this conference. I've already heard some advice I might want to incorporate. It's just a couple of paragraphs added and a few deleted or moved. I think the book would be better with them."

"I'd like to read the sample chapters in peace and quiet, then go over the outline again. And I want to know, after I do that, what you're planning to change. May I keep this overnight and meet with you again tomorrow?"

Jane said, "I'd be grateful."

"No promises, mind you. I think well of what I've seen so far. But I'd like to know more about the proposal before we discuss it. Would you mind giving me your room number?"

Jane managed to nod agreement without kissing the woman's feet. She all but floated out the door and went in search of Shelley.

Eleven

Jane was frantic to find Shelley and tell her all about her interview. She finally discovered Shelley sitting in the bar with Felicity. They each had a glass of red wine in front of them and were sharing a bowl of potato chips and a bowl of guacamole.

"Have you two been hiding from me?" Jane asked.

"Didn't you receive my message?" Shelley asked. "What do you think a cell phone is for?"

Jane pulled her phone out of her purse, looked at the little screen, and asked, "Is that what this little envelope thing means?" and added as the bartender passed, "A big glass of iced tea, please."

"The object, Jane," Shelley commented, "is to leave the phone on so you know when someone calls."

"I have been," Jane said, "but not when I'm in a seminar, and certainly not when I'm talking to an editor."

"Okay. You're right," Shelley said. This was something she rarely admitted to. "How did it go?"

"Wonderfully. She's a grown-up. She took the time to really read through the outline and a bit of the first chapter. I've given her a copy of the house plan and the village map, and she said she loved books with things like that."

She'd spoken calmly but what she really wanted to do was jump up and down with glee and hug everyone in sight. She knew that kind of behavior would make her look like a fool, especially in front of a professional writer.

"Congratulations," Felicity said. "I knew you'd like her."

"A bit early for congratulations," Jane said. "She also made it clear that she wasn't making any promises. I admitted I'd learned a few things here that I thought I might consider on a final pass. She's going to read the chapters and the outline tonight and contact me tomorrow about the changes I have in mind."

Jane's drink arrived and the three women decided to sit at a table at the back of the bar to finish the discussion. They carted their drinks, book bags, purses, potato chips, and guacamole along with them.

When they were finally seated, Shelley pulled a box out of her book bag. "Jane and I have a present for you, Felicity."

"Why?"

Jane said, "Because you've been very nice to us."

Shelley had even had the box gift wrapped. Felicity opened it and said, "Oh, how sweet of you both. It's a pin like Jane's." She put it on her jacket and they all admired it.

"Now tell us in detail every word and every look," Felicity said to Jane.

Jane did so.

"I'm glad to know you do know this might not work out," Felicity said. "Don't fail to go to your third interview. And would you make me a copy of your manuscript when you've made your final revisions? I'd really like to see the whole thing. If Melody Johnson doesn't take it for some reason, I might be able to make some other suggestions, if you'd like me to. Here's my card."

Jane's jaw nearly dropped.

"Shelley, we should have gotten this woman a far more expensive piece of jewelry," Jane said. "I'd love to have your comments, Felicity. That's so generous of you."

"Not really. I do like to help out unpublished writers if they've already had at least half a foot in a good door and show the right attitude toward what they're doing." She added, "Just so you don't tell any of the rest of the aspiring writers. I need to walk off this drink and brush my teeth or someone will start a rumor that I'm a lush," she finished, getting to her feet.

Before Felicity could leave, one of the conference planners approached her and took her aside. Jane and Shelley watched as Felicity kept shaking her head and saying "No."

Finally she caved in to the planner's plea and

came back to the table and said, "They've dragged me into the reviewers' panel. Zac Zebra has gone missing. He's not in his room. They've cruised all the meeting rooms and even the shops, and there's no sign of him. He lives nearby and they've even called him at home."

"But you're not a reviewer, are you?" Shelley asked. She didn't really care much that Zac had left the conference. As far as she knew, he was only there for his nuisance value.

"I used to be before I started writing. Then I found myself having to critique books by people who had become friends, or at least acquaintances, after I started being published. I wanted to be honest about their books. But I didn't want to criticize when a friend wrote a clunker. Even the best writers eventually write a bad book. So I quit reviewing. I didn't think anyone here knew about it. I was wrong about that."

"You'll make it through okay. Just tell the audience what you've just told us," Shelley suggested.

"I suppose that's all I can do," Felicity said. "It's odd, though, that Zac would be willing to miss a chance to show off."

"Maybe he's just lost his schedule and doesn't realize," Jane said.

When Felicity had gone, Jane said to Shelley, "This is the last seminar of the day, and I have my last appointment."

"I'll go to the reviewers' panel for you," Shelley said. "You'll be able to slip in for most of it after your interview. I think we should both show our support for Felicity. I liked what she said about why she quit reviewing. I think the audience will as well."

Jane's last interview was with another baby agent. Tiffany was an insecure young woman with a small though prestigious agency. She seemed more nervous than Jane was. She was seriously pregnant as well.

"Tell me a little about your book," she suggested faintheartedly, as if she'd come to the end of her rope.

"I have three chapters and an outline," Jane said, handing over her last packet.

The young woman took the packet but didn't open it. "Just talk about it. I'll look this over later."

Jane did her best to articulate what the book was about. The girl kept glancing at her watch while Jane spoke. Finally when the fifteen minutes were over, she said, "Well, that sounds interesting. I'll read your material on the way back to New York. I assume you've put your address and phone number in the packet."

"I have. Thank you for your time," Jane said, rising and putting her hand forward to shake. The girl put out a limp, damp paw and looked even more disconcerted.

Jane was disappointed, of course. She realized, as well, that she wouldn't like to work with such a wimpy person in any case. Maybe the girl would like the proposal and pass it on to her boss, who had a very good reputation, according to Felicity. It might work out if the boss liked it and wanted to handle Jane herself.

She didn't really hold out a serious hope of this happening. This baby agent would probably go on maternity leave within the next month, and the proposal would linger at the bottom of a closet or under six other manuscripts on a shelf until it yellowed at the edges.

She went to find where the last seminars of the day were being held, and as she was looking down at the map as she walked through the lobby, she literally stumbled into Mel VanDyne.

"Mel, why didn't you tell me you were a speaker?"

He grinned. "Hi, Janey. I wanted to surprise you. I'm doing a presentation on forensics, plus I've been commandeered to take over for Detective Jess Jones. He was supposed to do one of these talks tomorrow, but he's having his appendix out today."

"It's so nice to have you here," Jane said, putting her arm around his waist and giving him a kiss on the cheek. "The last seminar of the day is going on, and a friend I've made is speaking on the panel, unwillingly. Would you like to come along with me?"

"Why not? Are you having a good time?" he asked her as they strolled along. "You look good in that outfit. It's new, isn't it?"

"Thanks. It *is* new. I'm having a wonderful time. I had two appointments with agents and one with an editor. The first agent brushed me off. The second agent was a pregnant teenaged marshmallow. The editor seemed genuinely interested in the book," she said, suppressing the urge to giggle madly. "I've met a lot of interesting people. I'm glad you're here. I'll tell you all about it when it's over. How about dinner Monday night? Prepare yourself to say nothing but 'Oh dear' and 'That's great.' "

"I should be free," Mel said with a grin. "Let's go out somewhere nice where there's a comfortable booth so I can nap for a while."

They joined Shelley in the back of the seminar room, and within seconds Mel's cell phone buzzed quietly. He walked out of the room and didn't return.

"This is a bit of a bore," Shelley said in a near whisper. "Felicity was the best speaker. The rest are unbelievably pompous. How did your interview go?"

A woman sitting two rows ahead of them turned and glared at them. "I'm trying to hear the speakers," she snapped.

They glared back and moved across the aisle where no one was close enough to hear them.

"I don't suppose Miss Mystery is on the panel?" Jane said. "She'd blow her cover."

"Everybody's trying to figure out which attendee she is. So far as I know, nobody has a firm idea," Shelley said. "Apparently she's good at fading into the background and keeping her ear to the ground. I admit I've noticed a middle-aged woman who hangs out in the lobby pretending to read a book. Always sitting close to authors who are having private talks. She's my best guess. I'll show her to you the next time I spot her."

An idiotic question was being addressed to Felicity, so Jane and Shelley stopped chatting to listen politely to how she responded. Felicity spoke gracefully, then sat back to endure the rest of the hour.

So did Jane and Shelley.

When it was over at last, they drifted out the door and discussed what they'd do that evening. Dinner, according to the schedule, was "on your own." They presumed this was because the editors and agents would be taking their clients out to nice dinners. There were no specific plans for the rest of the attendees, except that two conference rooms had been made available for people to sit and chat about whatever they liked. This seemed deadly to both Jane and Shelley.

"Want to cab down to that seafood restaurant we went to near the Merchandise Mart, the one you liked so much?" Shelley asked.

"It's Friday night. Wouldn't it be too late to make a reservation?" Jane asked.

"We could try. Do you want to take Mel along? My treat."

"If I can find him. I wonder what that call was about."

"Ring him up on his cell phone and see."

Jane did so. He didn't answer, so she left a message. He rang back a few minutes later when they'd gone up to the suite.

"Somebody found a man bashed in the head in the parking lot behind the hotel," he said. "I think he's part of this conference. A weird-looking guy with striped hair."

"Zac Zebra!" Jane exclaimed.

"That's not what it says on his driver's license and car registration."

"Zac Zebra is a pseudonym. Is he in bad shape?"

"Out like a light. The medics say his pulse is good, his breathing is normal, and his pupils are fine, but he's out cold. They're loading him into the ambulance now."

"I don't suppose you're free to go to a nice dinner with us?"

"I probably will be. This isn't my case. I was just the closest detective to the site when the emergency call came in. They've assigned it to someone else."

"We'll try to make a reservation for three for seven o'clock. We're close enough to the restaurant so we don't have to leave until quarter of seven. Let us know. Let's take a cab, though. I don't want to drive in the dark yet in my new car, and your MG is too small for three of us."

"What's this about Zac?" Shelley said when Jane had hung up.

"He was knocked out in the parking lot behind the hotel," Jane said. "It's not Mel's case, so he can probably come with us. He said the medical people don't think Zac's in big trouble."

"Let's book the reservation, if we can, and go back down to the lobby to see if anyone knows more about this. Better yet, we can ask the concierge to make the reservation for us. They always have more clout."

Twelve

Mel was able to join them for dinner. "Nice place," he said when the waiter had shown him to their table.

"The last time I was here, I was lame, tired, and frustrated," Jane said. "The dinner really perked me up. What have you learned about Zac? And what is his real name?"

"Harold Spotswood. He was still unconscious last time I checked. But the doctors don't seem terribly alarmed. They've put him through all their machines. There's a hairline fracture, they said, but no pooling of blood or clotting in his brain. He appears to have just needed a good long nap, as I understand it."

Shelley studied her menu, not liking this sort of talk when she was about to eat. "Anything else you know about him?" she asked, hoping to escape from more medical talk.

"Just one weird thing. He was clutching a page from what appeared to be a very old paperback book," Mel said. "An old page with slightly yellow edges. What was his connection with this conference?"

"He's a book reviewer," Jane said. "Not at all a well-respected one. And a macho pig who only likes extremely hard-boiled books written by men."

"If he sticks with that, who's to care?" Mel asked.

"It's just that he also claims to read dozens of books a day," Jane said. "Our friend Felicity was telling us about him. He obviously doesn't read past the first few pages and makes enormous mistakes. He also takes potshots at women mystery writers. Felicity said he calls any mystery written by a woman a 'powder puff' book."

"I noticed when I went through the lobby that most of the people wearing those badges you had on were women," Mel said. "So why was he even invited to the conference?"

"Felicity says he goes to lots of mystery conferences blowing his own horn. It may be that some authors like him, even if he gets his facts wrong," Shelley explained. "After all, most people in the arts think any publicity is good publicity. Felicity also suggested that the planners thought a little conflict might be a good thing. I think I'll have the crab Louis salad."

She looked up and said, "Jane, you haven't even looked at your menu."

"I was thinking about that page from a book. Was he found in his car, Mel?"

"It looked as if he'd parked his van, turned off the ignition, and released his seat belt, and someone jerked open the door, bopped him on the back of the head, and threw him to the ground. The driver's-side door was standing open. We might be wrong about this though. It's just an initial impression. Why do you ask?"

"So it's possible he was reading some page of the book before coming back into the hotel? He might have clutched the page and accidentally ripped it out, right?"

"Possibly. Why does this interest you?"

"Yesterday he slipped up next to this very important editor and gave her a paperback book and whispered something to her. The editor looked startled. But she just handed it off to her assistant and dismissed Zac with a curt nod."

Shelley said, "Jane, I think he was probably just trying to put one of his old books into her hands to see if she'd republish it. Felicity told us he used to be a novel writer," she explained to Mel.

"What did he write?" Mel asked.

Both women shrugged. Jane said, "We don't know. We don't even know what name he used or what kind of novels they were. Felicity might know."

"Hmm," Mel said. Putting down the menu, he added, "I think I'll have the same thing Shelley's having. All I had at lunch was a greasy grilled cheese sandwich and a can of warm Dr Pepper. Crab Louis would erase the memory."

"Don't you want to talk to Felicity about Zac?" Jane asked.

"I may. But it's not my case. Give me her name when we return to the hotel and I'll pass it along to the guy in charge of it."

Shelley asked, "Was Zac robbed?"

"Apparently not," Mel said. "That's how we knew his name. He still had his wallet with lots of cash in it. Nobody even snatched the gold chains off his neck."

"Was the rest of the book in the van?" Jane said.

"I didn't look. Someone else might know."

The waiter was hovering impatiently. Mel and Shelley ordered their salads and Jane ordered grilled red snapper. Over dinner Jane gave Mel a short overview of people she'd met, the interviews, and which classes were interesting.

"Tomorrow the direction shifts," Shelley said. "Today was all writers, editors, and agents giving opinions. Tomorrow it's special presentations. Some touchy-feely stuff about getting in touch with your muse," she said with a disgusted shudder. "Also something called 'The Scene of the Crime'—that's probably what you're taking over, right?"

"Yup. I'm doing that and then later the forensic talk," Mel said. "What else goes on tomorrow?"

"Some off-the-premises trips," Jane said. "Volunteers are taking some people to the Field Museum, of course. Others are taking attendees to a botanical garden that has an expert on poisonous plants. There's also a class somewhere else about guns. What kinds, how to shoot with them."

Mel smiled at the image of all those women, most of them middle-aged, being carted off to learn how to kill people in their books.

"Why are you smirking?" Jane asked.

"No reason. I was just thinking of a joke someone made at the office this morning," he lied. "Not appropriate for delicate ears."

When they returned to the hotel, Jane had a message from Melody Johnson, the editor who had been encouraging.

"I've looked over your sample chapters and outline and would like to meet with you tomorrow. How does nine-thirty in the morning sound? Give me a call at room 602 to confirm."

Jane looked at her watch. It was nine thirty-seven. Probably that wasn't too late to call. Melody was presumably still out to dinner with her authors. Jane left a message confirming the time and asked where they should meet.

Mel had come up to see the suite and Shelley was showing him around while Jane was listening to and returning the phone message.

She found the two of them in Shelley's bathroom, Mel with his shoes off, testing the heated floor.

"Neat news," Jane said. "The editor wants to meet with me in the morning. I must make some notes about what I'd like to change about the plot to make it more of a mystery and about how I'd like to tone down some of the description of the house. What time are you speaking, Mel?"

"One o'clock," he said, putting his shoes back on.

"We'll be there to hear you," Jane said.

"There's no need," Mel said. "I don't want to interfere with your plans."

"But we want to hear you," Shelley said. "We'll be there."

"Janey," Mel said. "Get on with your preparations for the appointment. I'm going down to the bar and stay out of your way."

"I'll come with you, if you don't mind," Shelley said. "Jane needs to be left alone for a while."

Jane sat on her bed with the notebook that was one of the freebies included in the conference book bags. She wrote down everything that had been simmering in the back of her mind since the interview with Melody Johnson and the subsequent panels of speakers. It didn't take her long, so she called Mel's cell phone. "Would you like to come up here?" she asked.

He said, "Might as well. Shelley's found someone else to talk to."

She greeted him at the door. He threw his jacket on a chair and followed her to her room. She'd already gathered up her papers and disappeared into the bathroom. When she came out, naked, she said, "The floor is heating up. I've set all the shower jets at a nice warm level. Let's play in there."

Shelley came back at eleven, saw Mel's jacket on the chair, and quietly went to her own room without disturbing Jane.

Mel left at one in the morning, in spite of Jane's objections. "I'm supposed to be in my room. And you need to be up early for your meeting."

Shelley and Jane were both wide-awake at seven. Melody Johnson called Jane back shortly after eight, saying she hoped she wasn't calling too early and suggesting that they meet in her hotel room, where they could speak privately. Jane agreed and quickly hopped into the shower. When she came back out, room service had brought up the simple breakfast Shelley had ordered for the two of them.

"Are you ready for your interview?" Shelley asked.

"Yes. I've made quite a lot of notes. I won't bother her with all of them unless she asks to hear them. I've put the most important changes up front in my notes."

"I'm so excited for you," Shelley said, spreading raspberry jam onto a hot Wolferman's muffin.

"Don't become too excited. It's not a slam dunk," Jane said.

"I know that. But I have a good feeling about it. Shall we go to the first presentation this morning? It's at eight-thirty."

"I might as well sit in for a few minutes, since we've paid for it," Jane said.

Thirteen

Jane had awakened that morning excited about the meeting with the editor. She was well prepared. She knew now that she'd finished the book as a mystery. She hadn't started it, though, with anything mysterious. It was a matter of making clear there was something that was troubling Priscilla from the first chapter, and at intervals along the way. She'd even marked on her outline where these intervals were.

But in the back of her mind, rattling around, was the vague thought that she should have asked Mel something else about Zac. She closed her eyes, remembering what he'd said at dinner, but it was no help. It was a query that had flitted across her mind and vaporized instantly while he was describing the scene of the crime.

From experience she knew, or at least hoped, it would come to her when she least expected it. Halfway through a ham sandwich. Or when she was brushing her teeth or peeling potatoes. She'd

often had lost memories pop up at that kind of
boring time.

Once, when someone had asked her who was
the artist who did the sculptures and pictures of
horses, Jane had had the name on the tip of her
tongue for days. When she was loading the dishwasher, thinking about what she'd have for
lunch, she had found herself shouting "Frederic
Remington" out of the blue.

That time she'd nearly dropped the glass she
was putting on the top shelf. And she'd scared
Max and Meow half to death as they were weav-
ing around her feet in hopes of her dropping
food.

She wouldn't try to force whatever was puz-
zling her about Zac right now.

"Are you ready?" Shelley called out from the
enormous parlor.

"I am. What are the choices at the eighty-thirty
session?"

"I don't remember," Shelley said as she was
making sure the door to the suite had caught and
locked. "Do you have that booklet they gave us
with the schedule?"

Jane looked in her book bag. "Nope. I must
have left it on the bedside table."

"Then we'll do our sit-where-we-can-escape
deal."

The eight-thirty session turned out to be a combi-
nation of two things—neither one to their taste

The first was the speech that the allegedly boring speaker was supposed to give the day before except that Sophie Smith had usurped all his time. The other was another hit at grammar.

Jane and Shelley slipped out.

They went to the restaurant in the hotel and had coffee and luscious croissants with real butter and raspberry jam. "I'm glad I brought along my water pick," Jane said. "I don't want to go to this interview with seeds stuck in my teeth."

Shelley glanced at her watch. "Only forty-five minutes from now. You're ready, of course."

Jane just rolled her eyes and took another croissant and slathered it generously with butter and raspberry jam.

When she went to Melody Johnson's room, she discovered that it was a small suite. Melody had Jane's outline spread out on the dining table. Jane pulled her copy of the outline out of her book bag and they sat down, Melody sitting at the side of the table and Jane at the head. It turned out, fortunately, that much of what they had each marked on the outline tallied almost exactly. They were both pleased.

"Phew," Melody said. "I was afraid you were unaware that the mystery didn't really start until three-quarters through the book. We've both moved pretty much the same bits of the plot further forward in the manuscript. I gave you my

card earlier, didn't I? Please send this to me as
soon as you finish the revisions."

"I'm glad you didn't see the whole thing. I forgot bathrooms in the description of the house
and then researched it to death and put in far too
many details about bathrooms at the time the
book is set," Jane said. "That's one of the most
valuable bits of advice I've learned here. To do a
lot of research and then use only the unusual
parts that most people wouldn't know about. All
I'm keeping is the part about the cisterns on the
roofs that were used to collect the water for
flushing."

"Really? That is interesting."

They both gathered up their papers and shook
hands. Melody said, "You do realize I'm not
promising anything. The marketing people sometimes take a great dislike to something an editor
likes enormously, and they have more clout than
editors do."

"That's another thing I've learned here," Jane
said. "I'm so glad I came to this conference and
glad, too, to have met you."

Jane had spent quite a long time with Melody
Johnson, and when she went in search of Shelley,
Shelley reminded her that Chester Griffith's ten-
thirty talk started in only five minutes. This was
one seminar Jane had really wanted to hear. He
was the bookseller that Felicity had told them
about who knew virtually everything about

women mystery writers and liked their work better than hard-boiled men's books.

"You can tell me all about your interview with Ms. Johnson after the talk. I want to hear it, too," Shelley said.

They hurried to find good seats close to the front. The speech was, indeed, fascinating. Chester not only could quote from almost every book he'd ever read, but he'd also learned what Jane had learned: Do your research and don't bore listeners and readers by telling them what they already know.

Jane and Shelley both took copious notes. He mentioned several authors he highly recommended that neither woman had read. It would mean one more trip to the booksellers' room, specifically to Mr. Griffith's booth before it was out of those books.

Jane whispered to Shelley, "The account of my interview will have to wait while we buy some of these books he's talked about."

"You're sure that's okay with you? I don't want you to forget to repeat every word Ms. Johnson told you," Shelley whispered back.

"I haven't forgotten anything. I probably won't put it in the right order though."

When the talk was over, they nearly ran to the booksellers' room. Mr. Griffith did have a few old copies of the out-of-print books as well as new ones he'd talked about, and they snatched them and held on to them until he could return to sell them.

"I vaguely remember reading and liking Dorothy Simpson's and Gwendoline Butler's books with the British detectives long ago. But I need to catch up on their later work. I just forget, somehow, to look under B and S in the bookstores, I guess. I'm so glad he mentioned them."

"I want to try out Deborah Crombie. I liked what he said about her work. I don't think I've ever read one of hers," Shelley came back.

When Mr. Griffith returned to his booth, they both thanked him for his suggestions, then took another heavy hit on their credit cards.

"Let's take these up to the suite and then have lunch so you can tell me about your interview. We have time before Mel's presentation," Shelley suggested. "Then we can go back to dipping into our new stash of books."

Fourteen

Jane didn't really expect Mel to tell the audience much more than he had already told her about his work. She was attending in a supportive role, providing him with a friend and lover in the audience. She was surprised, however, at how much she learned about investigation of the scene of the crime. This was a genuinely enlightening talk and drew a great many more attendees than she'd seen in the other room. People were standing at the sides of the room and sitting in the middle of the center aisle.

All of them, including Jane, were taking notes. It was a good thing she and Shelley had come early and found seats in the front row. Jane was so proud of him she couldn't stop grinning. It was a new impression of him—as a public speaker who was so skilled.

However, he did go on for just a bit too long about how it was all too easy these days to acquire thin latex gloves to conceal fingerprints.

Every hardware store, beauty supply shop, and paint store provided them.

Then he admitted that the occasional really stupid criminal sometimes disposed of them near the scene after committing the crime. When that happened, the gloves could be carefully turned inside out to reveal the prints.

"But it doesn't happen often enough," he added with a dazzling smile, then went right into a discussion of fiber matches.

After he was done with the speech, at least twenty attendees, mostly older women, lined up to ask him specific questions. Jane and Shelley stayed in their seats until he'd answered all of them.

"You were great!" Jane said when everyone had left, and she gave him a big hug. "I had no idea what a good speaker you are, and how good you look at a podium."

"It's all part of my job," he said modestly.

"No. Lots of people in law enforcement know what you know. Not many of them can present it as well," Jane insisted.

"Thanks," he said, looking slightly embarrassed at this sudden gush of praise.

"What are you doing for the rest of the day?" Shelley asked him. "Are you going to attend any of the other sessions?"

"Nope. Fictional crime isn't really my interest," he admitted. "The few novels I've read have glaring mistakes that drive me crazy.

That's why we send officers out to explain to the public how sophisticated and technical the process really is these days. Besides, I'm giving the talk about forensics I was supposed to do in the first place."

"Have you heard anything else about Zac?" Jane asked.

"Just that he's conscious. No apparent brain damage."

"That's good," Jane replied. "But does he know what happened to him?"

"Not a clue, if you'll forgive the phrase. I'm told he remembers that he needed to do something at his home, which is apparently fairly close. Nothing after that."

"Will he remember later, do you think?" Shelley asked.

"I'm not qualified to answer that, as you both know. Sometimes a blow to the head only creates temporary amnesia. Sometimes it's permanent. I'm not a doctor and don't play one on TV."

"Wait just one more minute, Mel," Jane said, closing her eyes, hoping she could remember the fleeting, and now missing, question she wanted to ask Mel about Zac. She still couldn't pull it from the back of her brain. She knew it was there somewhere, if only she could dredge it up.

"Never mind. I've lost the thought again," Jane said.

Mel was obviously becoming impatient, if not downright cranky, about being held up to discuss an attack that he'd already said several times wasn't his case.

Jane said too cheerfully, "You could collect a bunch more accolades if you'd hang out in the lobby for a while."

"What was that about?" Shelley asked when Mel had gone.

"What?"

"You acted as if you had a question to ask him."

"I thought I did. But I couldn't remember what the question was. I felt for a second there that it was about to bubble up when Mel finished. It passed fleetingly through my mind yesterday, but I can't seem to be able to bring it back. I think it might have been important."

"Any way I can help?" Shelley asked.

"No. It's a Frederic Remington thing."

"What on earth does that mean?"

"You know. When you're trying desperately to remember someone's name? And when you give up, it comes to you out of the blue a couple of days later and just springs out at you."

"This happens to you often?" Shelley said with a worried look.

"It happens to everybody, I thought. I've seen you suddenly come out with a word you'd been searching your mind for. Last time it happened, it was 'ontology,' whatever that is. Remember saying it to yourself in the middle of a conversation about petunias?"

Shelley had the grace to admit it. "I guess I see what you mean. Sort of. And it was dahlias, not petunias."

"What are we doing the rest of the day?" Jane asked.

"Shopping until Mel's next session?"

Jane replied, "I'm shopped out and you know how surly I can become when I reach that point. There's a mystery trivia contest in the next session. Want to sit in on it with me?"

"No, thanks. I haven't read half the mysteries you have. I don't go places where I'm bound to feel stupid," Shelley said. "Isn't there some sort of awards party tonight? And a dinner we paid for in our fees?"

"If I'm remembering right, it's just a snack-and-drink thing. I wish one of us had brought along the schedule. The registration booth is closed temporarily, and the only way to get one is to steal someone else's. Why don't you go up to the suite and find one and make our plans for the rest of the conference? We're both free now to do whatever we want. Although I'd really rather leave and go home and work on my book after Mel's second talk."

"Jane, don't say that. Not only have you paid for the whole conference, there might still be things you can learn that will be useful."

"Maybe you're right," Jane admitted. "I'll stick it out." She added wistfully, "I just wish I could remember . . ."

"Stop working at remembering whatever it was. Your subconscious won't be forced to disgorge it until it's ready. Think about something else. Like dahlias."

The mystery trivia contest was fun and clever. It was run by Chester Griffith, the bookseller who knew so much about virtually every book he'd ever read. Jane had so much enjoyed his earlier presentation and was looking forward to this one.

At first it was easy. He'd recite a short paragraph from a mystery novel. The first person to raise his or her hand would be allowed to answer. The contest was on the honor system.

The first two questions contained the name of the sleuth. You received one point for identifying the author right. If you knew the title of the book, you earned an extra ten points. If you also knew the first date of publication, you'd tally up another twenty points. Almost all of the participants knew who the author was on the first question. It was Ngaio Marsh because Griffith chose a paragraph that mentioned Roderick Alleyn. Even Jane knew that one. Another half dozen, including Jane, knew which book it was from, *"Black as He's Painted."*

Only one participant guessed the right publishing year, and she was an attractive, though somewhat overweight, young woman at the very back of the room. Several guessed the decade. Jane failed utterly on this part, though she thought it was probably in the fifties because it involved a black African friend Alleyn had been in school with and was surprisingly politically correct for the time it was written.

The next question was easy as well. Miss Marple was named in the paragraph, and Jane knew it was the first Agatha Christie book to feature Miss Marple but couldn't remember the title, though she remembered quite a bit of the plot.

Again, the young woman at the back of the room had the name of the author, the name of the book, and only missed the publication date by one year. Many of the participants also remembered the title.

The third quote was a little bit harder. It didn't mention the sleuth's name, but gave his sidekick's name instead. Many of them knew the author immediately. Even Jane, and only because she'd dipped into one of the Dorothy Simpson books she'd purchased the day before. The sidekick was Mike Lineham, Luke Thanet's assistant.

Nobody except the young woman at the back of the room knew which title it was, and even she didn't come up with a date of publication.

The quotes became progressively harder and harder to identify. Every now and then one happened to come from one of the participants' very favorite mystery, and a few of them gained on the young woman's score.

Jane eventually gave up trying to guess when

it came down to mention of minor continuing characters, like the usual pathologist in the series. She was awfully glad that Shelley had taken a pass on coming to this event. Shelley would have been completely at sea and mad as the dickens about it.

By the end of the forty-five-minute session, the quotes were so obscure that practically nobody had any answers. Even the young woman who'd started out so brilliantly was stymied by a few of the last questions. But she did win the contest. Chester Griffith presented her with a rare mystery of Wilkie Collins's and asked her to introduce herself. Jane vaguely recognized the book, which had been in a glass cabinet in the booksellers' room and labeled for sale for over a hundred dollars.

"I'm LaLane Jones. I teach a writing class in a college here in town on the history of the mystery genre and the science fiction genre."

There were groans from the rest of the audience and a few good-natured remarks about this not being fair. LaLane Jones admitted it with a laugh.

Jane thought about her as she went back to the suite. As much as Jane herself enjoyed mysteries, she had no desire to be an expert on them the way Ms. Jones did. She wondered if Ms. Jones, as young and attractive as she was, had a real life. She hoped so.

But doubted it.

This made Jane a bit sad, and she tried to cheer

herself back up by thinking how nice it had been that neither the dreadful Vernetta nor Gaylord had bothered to attend.

That, at least, was a valuable perk. Maybe they'd even gone home.

Fifteen

Mel's second speech was even better than the first because he'd had plenty of time to prepare it. After it was done, his cell phone rang again and he took the call, then told Jane that he was leaving the hotel without staying the second night.

"That call didn't have something to do with Zac, did it?" Jane asked.

"No. It's a simple shoplifting a few doors down from here. I'm back on duty."

On the one hand, Jane hated to see him go. On the other hand, she was hoping that there would still be something interesting to learn if she stuck out the rest of the conference.

Unfortunately, the Strausmanns hadn't gone home. At the snack supper Vernetta was dressed as Dorothy from the Wizard of Oz and Gaylord was adorned with sheets of aluminum foil, pasted together with duct tape, being the Tin Man.

"They should be locked up in some institution," Shelley said. "At least Vernetta should. Gaylord made the mistake of sitting down and has already split the back of his pants and looks deeply embarrassed. Poor man. Those are some flashy undies he's wearing."

"Rich man, you mean," Jane said. "He's going to live in his wife's mansion and drive a Mercedes. He might even buy a flock of them in every color. Letting himself be made a fool in public isn't such a high price to pay."

"I'll bet he becomes fed up with it soon," Shelley predicted. "I'd bet good money that he runs off with a shy, blonde, seventeen-year-old anorexic bimbo within a year. Maybe two years. He'll probably be allowed to keep ownership of half the house and all of the cars."

"Do you really think so?"

"I can but hope," Shelley said. "Let's go to a real dinner. I can't bear to be in the same room with these people."

"Okay by me," Jane said. As they were heading for the nicest of the hotel restaurants, she said, "I don't understand it. Vernetta doesn't even know how to speak English. And I'd guess she has no idea how to spell anything over four letters long. She's so utterly ignorant about human nature. Except her own, of course. How could she possibly write a good novel? It seems to me that making up characters that seem real, especially if they're nothing like the writer who creates them, is the essence of fiction."

"That's exactly what I've been wondering. I

wonder if it simply has a lot of really good sex scenes."

"Shelley!" Jane exclaimed. "Do you really suppose so?"

Shelley shrugged. "Who could guess? Maybe we should look it up if it's still somewhere on the Internet."

"I don't think I could stand to read it," Jane said. "Good sex scenes or not. Come to think of it, we don't even know where to look. I've never heard what it's titled. I wonder if Felicity knows. She hasn't read it but she said some of her friends had attempted to wade through it. Anyway, since it's been sold to a real publisher, it's probably been removed from the site, wouldn't you imagine?"

"Maybe so. I think this obsession with costumes means something," Shelley speculated.

"Like what?"

"Maybe she has a fabulous imagination hidden under her horrible public personality?"

"She's simply an obsessive show-off. Her imagination only runs to crummy costumes," Jane claimed.

As they entered the dining room, Jane spotted someone way back in the corner waving to them. "There's Felicity. She seems to be inviting us to join her."

They told the waiter to take them to her table.

"What's up?" Jane asked, afraid it was just a friendly wave, not an actual invitation, when she noticed that Felicity had an old book open on the table.

"Nothing much. It's just too dark in here to read this tiny print, and I'd rather visit with you two. I haven't even ordered anything but a drink yet. You were just in time."

"We didn't see you at the snack party," Jane said.

"I figured Vernetta might turn up."

They regaled Felicity with the Dorothy and Tin Man description. "He'd already burst out of his costume and was wearing really fancy underwear," Jane said.

"No!" Felicity said with a vulgar laugh. She closed her book—an ancient Mary Stewart paperback—and set it beside her at the edge of the table, and it promptly fell to the floor.

"Let me pick it up for you," Jane said.

"No, I can grab it," Felicity said. She leaned over, still laughing, and remained unseen for an unusually long time. She finally came back upright with the book in one hand and several loose pages of it in the other.

"Glue's gone. I'll put the pages in order later."

"That's it!" Jane exclaimed so loudly that several people looked around at her.

"What is?" Shelley asked.

"Old paperbacks often have pages that come loose," Jane said, lowering her voice. "That's why Zac was holding one when he was attacked. That's what I've been meaning to ask Mel about all this time."

"Why?" Shelley inquired.

"Because it might mean something."

"Like what?"

"Your handsome detective is in charge of this case but he still gave his talks?" Felicity wasn't quite grasping what this was about. It was certainly more interesting than Gaylord's underwear.

"No," Jane said, surprising Shelley that she'd paid attention in spite of her deer-in-the-headlights look. "He was just called first because he was the closest. It's some other detective's case."

"Okay. I grasp that now," Felicity said. "But what does this have to do with the pages of old paperbacks falling out?"

"Mel mentioned in passing that Zac was found on the ground just outside his van. He had an old yellowed book page in his hand. That's what I was trying so hard to remember."

Shelley said, "Why is this so important to you, Jane, that you've fretted so much about recalling it?"

Jane shrugged. "I don't know exactly. I just have a strong feeling that it might be significant."

"Nonsense," Shelley said briskly. "He was probably waiting for someone and reading while he waited. Maybe he dropped it like Felicity did and was trying to find where to put it back in when he was attacked."

"I know that makes sense," Jane admitted. "It's

probably true, too. Somehow I had an idea it might have more of a meaning."

Both the other women were trying hard not to roll their eyes in disbelief at this bizarre remark.

"Where was the rest of the book?" Jane said. "Mel didn't mention a book being in the van."

"Why would he mention it anyway?" Shelley asked. "Probably half of the people attending this conference have books in their cars if they drove here. You yourself have already stashed some of your own in your new Jeep so you don't have to carry them all out at once, and I've loaded about half mine into the minivan."

Felicity said, "I've already shipped some of mine home through the hotel's office center."

"You're both right again," Jane said. "But still . . . would you order the shrimp pasta and iced tea for me while I go in the lobby and call Mel? I hate to see people making their phone calls from restaurant tables."

As Jane left, Felicity said, "If she feels so strongly about this, she could be right."

Shelley replied, "It's just writer's imagination." She added with a kind smile, "You have it, too."

Mel was even more skeptical than Shelley. "A page from a book? Yeah, I think I noticed that. I'd forgotten about it. Why are you asking?"

"It could be important. Were there other books in the vehicle?"

"I have no idea. Why do you think it's impor-
ant?"

"I'm not certain. I simply think it could be significant. Would you ask the detective in charge if
he could fax the page to the hotel? I have the
number here."

"Jane, get a grip. Why would anyone have
bothered keeping the page he had in his hand?"

"You don't mean when a person is attacked all
the relevant bits and pieces aren't kept? That
doesn't sound like what you said in the 'Scene of
the Crime' talk you gave."

"But he wasn't murdered. Just roughed up.
Nothing was even stolen," Mel objected. "And in
case you want to know, the hospital already re-
eased him this afternoon."

"Please, Mel. See if someone has the page. It
would mean a lot to me."

Mel sighed deeply. "Jane, I must have some
halfway decent reason for asking for this stupid
page. I can't just say 'a friend of mine would like
to see it.' "

"Why not? If it's still around and nobody
thinks it means anything, why wouldn't they let
someone see it?"

"Jane, you're the most meddling woman in the
world."

"I know that," she said, smiling. He'd caved.

She came back to the table and didn't mention
anything else about the page or her conversation

with Mel. And neither of the other women
brought it up. They just chatted about the conference and complained once again, halfheartedly
about Vernetta and Gaylord.

"Have you discovered any additional information about who Miss Mystery is?" Jane asked
Felicity.

"Not for sure. I have a theory though. I think
it's that woman who eavesdrops everywhere she
goes. In fact, she's sitting over there." Felicity
pointed with her hand close to the table. "The
plump one at the third table to the right with the
upswept gray hair and the purple suit. Keep an
eye on her. She's sitting next to a bunch of authors and making notes behind her menu so they
don't see her doing it."

Shelley said excitedly, "It's the same woman I
was guessing. Remember when I pointed her out
to you earlier, Jane? Great minds think alike."

Sixteen

As Jane, Shelley, and Felicity left the restaurant, Jane remembered to ask Felicity about Vernetta's e-pubbed book. "Is it still up on the Internet somewhere?"

"I have no idea. Interesting question though. She probably didn't even know to copyright it, much less remove it from wherever it is."

"Do you know the title of it?" Shelley asked. "Jane says she never wants to read it, but I'm curious."

"Someone told me the title," Felicity responded, "but I'm sorry, I don't remember what it was. Something with a word like 'Quest' in it. Finding someone? Searching?"

Shelley interrupted with another insight. "Isn't it odd that Vernetta and Gaylord don't brag about the book or the story? All that Vernetta seems interested in is bragging about the money she's made or will make."

Jane said, "I'd never realized that, but it's true.

How much of an advance did she receive? Do you know?"

Felicity frowned. "That I do recall vividly. A cool million. Of course, the publisher will spread it out as far as they can and try to make it up by making a movie deal to earn back the money."

"That's interesting," Shelley remarked. "Does Sophie Smith often pay that much for anyone's book? As cranky as she sounds, I assumed she'd be stingy as well."

"She is stingy. When I was with her the first time, it was all promises of bestsellerdom, but my part of the deal was to buckle down and produce the book in four months and take a rock-bottom advance so the publisher's money could all go into promotion. Lots of blah-blah about how it's a good idea to plan your income this way—drawing it out for as long a time as possible to save or bumping yourself into a higher tax rate all in one year and making horribly high social security contributions."

"Doesn't the publisher pay half of your social security like other businesses do?" Shelley asked.

"They most certainly don't. And they don't give you any retirement benefits either. The author has to pay it all. What's more, on my royalty statements they always have more returns from Canada than the number of books they claimed to have shipped."

Now Shelley had the stunned look, too surprised to even speak.

"I presume it didn't make you rich?" Jane asked.

"What do you think? No. I never even earned out the pitiful advance. I was young and stupid then. It was only my second book. I had a wimpy agent who was afraid to tackle someone as powerful as Sophie. Sophie even forgot to put any mention of my book in the sales booklet for the month it was released. And to answer your first question, Shelley, she often pays authors a bundle. But those people are the ones who are already highly successful. Many are merely unhappy with something about the publisher they're with. She lures them away with lots of money, then treats them as badly as she treats everyone else."

She did a little shake like a dog does when it's wet. "I shouldn't complain. I'm now with a good agent and good publisher and make a very comfortable living on my advances and royalties. Even though I have to turn over outrageous amounts of it to the IRS in estimated payments."

"You deserve it," Jane said, changing the subject as quickly as she could. She didn't want Shelley to go off on her own highly inflammatory opinions of the Internal Revenue Service.

As they were drawing apart to go their separate ways, Shelley said, "Oh, Felicity, would you ask around and see if you can find out what the e-bubbed version of Vernetta's book is called? I'm curious."

"I will. I promise. My payment to you for letting me vent. I think two of the people who claimed to have read it are here at the conference. I'll make a point of hunting them down."

Jane went to the front desk and asked if they'd received a fax for her of the page Zac was clutching in his hand when he was found. They hadn't. She feared that the page had simply been thrown away. She tried to tell herself she was being silly thinking the page meant anything at all. Although she was still convinced that it might have some significance.

She and Shelley went up to the suite to read for a while. The two evening seminars that were going on sounded useless. One was another one about grammar. The other was about costumes. On the way upstairs, Jane had stopped by the room where the costume seminar was to take place and picked up the handout that listed reference books and what periods of time they covered. That was all she wanted to know. She supposed the speaker would simply go through this sheet and explain endlessly what was already on the list.

She and Shelley made another run at the books they'd collected. Jane realized that two of them were by the woman Felicity said was a wonderful friend who, unfortunately, let her character go stupid and put herself in danger at the end of each book. Jane wondered if the bookseller might let her return it in trade for something else she'd like better.

She put the question to Shelley, who replied, "I'd guess the bookseller would if it was still in good shape. You haven't broken the spine yet, have you?"

This was one of the points that Jane and Shelley disagreed about. Shelley felt that books should remain in good condition forever. Jane's feeling was that if she'd paid for it, it was hers to abuse if she chose. Shelley had often come to Jane's house and seen a book squashed open, face down, on a counter or over the arm of a chair. "Buy book-marks, Jane!" she always said.

"Waste of money. I usually try to use something like a grocery receipt," Jane would counter. "If it's my book, I can do anything I want with it. I could tear pages out to wash windows. Take it into the bathtub and know it might come back out wet. Or put it in the trash if I'm not liking it."

She'd never let Shelley find out that the reference books she'd purchased for working on her book were highlighted in yellow throughout. That would have put Shelley completely over the brink.

The phone rang and Jane was closest. "Yes, thank you. I'll be right down to pick it up," she said to the caller.

"What was that about?" Shelley asked.

"I have a fax at the front desk. Mel must have found the page Zac was hanging on to," Jane explained. "I'll be right back."

When she returned to the suite and opened the

envelope, she was disappointed. She knew Mel said it was an old page with yellow edges. Unfortunately, the yellow turned into gray when faxed. The words on the outside edge were virtually unreadable. She sat down with a pencil at the dining table and tried to puzzle out what the missing words were.

Shelley was pointedly ignoring her. She was buzzing around picking things up and putting them away. She finally broke down after twenty minutes when there was no longer anything to move or clean up. "Is it interesting?"

"Not especially. It's grammatically correct is the best I can say for it. It's a guy named Malachi thinking over why it seems to be so important to him to find a woman he's only seen in a dream that he's had several times. I'd wonder the same thing if I were he, but wouldn't fret myself about it."

"So it's not worthwhile," Shelley said in a voice of triumph.

"Who knows?" Jane said. "Maybe the rest of it was really good." The phone rang again. This time Shelley picked it up. "Let me write that down. Jane, where's a notepad and pencil?"

"You put everything that wasn't nailed down away somewhere," Jane said. She handed Shelley a paperback book and a pen from her purse and said, "Write it down on the first page."

"No. I'd ruin the book."

"Suit yourself," Jane said, not wishing for another round of how-a-book-must-be-treated.

With great reluctance, Shelley wrote something on the reverse side of the back cover.

"That was Felicity," she said. "The title of Vernetta's e-pubbed book is *Martin's Quest* or *The Quest of a Martian*, she said. Two different people called it by different names."

"I doubt the Martian one," Jane said with a smile. "I can't imagine Sophie Smith paying a fortune for a science fiction book."

Seventeen

"It's odd about this page Zac was holding," Jane said.

"What's odd?"

"Many books these days have a heading on each page. You know, the author's name at the top of one page and the title of the book on the opposite page."

Shelley checked some of the books she'd purchased. "You're right. I never noticed that. But this page doesn't," she said, looking over Jane's shoulder.

"If we can't hunt down Zac or if he doesn't remember what the book was, we'll never know."

"Will we care?" Shelley asked.

"I think so. I don't think that Sophie Smith's illness was natural, nor was the attack on Zac. Either one could have died."

"You amaze me. You don't think they were just pranks? And Sophie could have just eaten a bad egg with her breakfast."

Jane said, "If you were eating a bad egg, you'd know it right away."

"I just meant it as an example," Shelley said grumpily.

"I think these two 'unfortunate' events are connected. Remember that Zac handed Sophie a book at the reservation desk. It must be the connection."

"Did she then give it back to him and he was looking it over when he was attacked?"

"Maybe," Jane claimed. "Or it was another copy."

Jane suddenly slapped her head. "I know who might be able to identify it!"

"Identify what?"

"The page from the book Zac was reading. Or at least holding." She went on to explain about the contest Chester Griffith had conducted, and the woman who won the prize. "She's a teacher at a local college and teaches about the mystery and science fiction genres. Her name is . . ."

Jane screwed up her eyes and tried to bring the woman's name up. "Mr. Griffith will remember," she finally said. "I'm going down to the desk and have copies of the page made. Maybe if they lighten it up a bit, the words at the end will be easier to decipher."

"I'll come with you," Shelley said, somewhat to Jane's surprise. It was the first hint that Shelley was accepting Jane's wobbly theory that the page meant something.

"Make me a copy," Shelley said when they arrived at the front desk.

"Why?"

"I'm not telling," Shelley replied.

Jane went to find Chester Griffith. He was still at his book booth and was engaged with a collector who was arguing over the price of a rare book. Jane had to wait impatiently for the conversation to end, which it did with the customer accepting Griffith's choice of cost.

"I'm sorry to bother you . . ."

"You're not a bother. You're a good customer," Chester said with a smile.

"I'm trying to remember the name of the young woman who won the contest, and I know your memory is better than mine," Jane said with a smile.

"She's LaLane Jones."

"Of course," Jane said. "All I could recall was that the first name had two 'L' sounds. Do you think she's still in the hotel somewhere?"

"I should think so. She's on the list of attendees on the back of the program."

"I've lost my program," Jane admitted.

Chester leaned down and pulled an extra program from a hidden shelf. "I always receive a couple of extra ones."

"Thank you so much," she said. She headed for the closest house phone and asked to be connected to guest LaLane Jones.

The phone rang twice and a woman's voice said, "Hello?"

"Is this Ms. LaLane Jones?"

"Yes, it is."

"I'm Jane Jeffry, one of the people attending the conference. I admired how much you knew about mysteries. I need to pick your brain, which I know to be an amazing storehouse. I was hoping you'd meet me somewhere, in a location of your choice."

"How about the book room? Give me about ten minutes."

"This is so mysterious," Ms. Jones said when Jane snagged her and introduced herself. "What do you need to know and why?"

"Let's sit down somewhere quiet," Jane said, indicating a sofa in the corner of the room that was currently not in use by other readers. She handed the copies of the front and back of the page to LaLane Jones.

"I'm hoping you'll recognize these two pages. I'll keep as quiet as a mouse while you read them. And then I'll tell you why I need to learn who wrote it."

Jane sat, as she promised, silently. She didn't look at LaLane for fear of making her nervous. Instead she studied the other shoppers. They were all fully engaged in looking for new or old books and handling them gently and respectfully. Jane wondered if some of them were like her, and once having purchased a book they felt they could treat it as their own. Breaking the spine so they could spread it and read while eating, holding the page open with a knife with a touch of mayonnaise on it.

"I have a very vague memory of reading this," LaLane finally said. It's good that it's page 25 and 26. I think that's about as far as I read. It bored me senseless."

"Me, too," Jane said. "Do you know who wrote it?"

"I might. It was a man, of course. That was back in the days when only men wrote science fiction. Or at least sold it. I've always suspected that some of the writers were women pretending to be men. Now it's different. Some women are at the top of the heap. I keep a book list that's always with me. I may have a record."

"For a book you didn't even want to read clear through?" Jane asked.

LaLane smiled. "Those are sometimes the most important ones to jot down, so you don't pick up another one by the same writer. Come up to my room and let's see if I can figure it out."

As LaLane opened the small case containing the records of her reading, Jane realized how truly obsessive the woman was.

"I think I read this when I'd broken my right wrist and couldn't write very well." She picked up the relevant notebook and started flipping pages. "Yes, here we are. I can hardly read my own handwriting. It was titled something like *Martin's* or *Marvin's Quest*. By James Cuttler, I think. I gave it an F minus."

"Do you know who James Cuttler is?"

"I could make a guess, I suppose. It must have been one of about six or seven who kept changing names. There were a lot of hack writers back then turning books out under a great many pseudonyms."

"Could it have been Zac Zebra?" Jane asked.

"Without the copyright page, I wouldn't know. But I know he once wrote under a number of names. Only three books, as I recall. Each of them more dreadful than the last and with a different publisher. Now it's time for you to explain why you're asking."

"Fair enough. I guess you know Zac was attacked yesterday."

"I heard that, but it must not have been all that violent. I understand he's already back here somewhere."

"When he was found in the parking lot, this page was in his hand."

"How strange," LaLane Jones said. "I wonder why that was."

"I have a theory. It's from a very old book and the glue must have been fragile. Maybe he was going through the book after the page fell out to put it back where it belonged."

"Possibly. I can't imagine anyone but the author himself being interested in reading this. What an interesting mystery this has turned out to be. Why don't you ask Zac yourself? And be sure to let me know what he says."

"That's the very next thing I'd planned to do. I'll report back to you, I promise."

Jane went back up to the suite. Shelley was reading the copy of the page. "I have an idea," she said. She'd underlined one sentence.

"What is it?"

Shelley still wouldn't say. "I may be wrong, and if so, I won't ever tell you what it was. Let's have a good dinner and not talk about this anymore tonight."

They took their programs down to the restaurant to study them and plan the next day. "I don't see much of anything that hasn't already been covered," Jane said. "Someone might have another view of some topic that we've already heard though. Frankly, I think this conference is at least one day too long. I'd like to go home."

"No, you won't. We've paid for the whole thing and we're going to stick it out," Shelley insisted. "We want to squeeze out our money's worth."

After dinner they went back to the suite and both sat around reading some of the books that they hadn't already taken to their cars. Jane went to bed early and had the weirdest dream. It was so vivid that she woke up in the middle of night sweating.

It was a version of a jungle movie she'd once watched partway through. It was a violent and awful movie, but there was a special effect that really impressed her. The bad guy, who was some sort of monster, wasn't pictured in the normal way. He was made of panes of clear glass. When he stood still, you couldn't even see him. But when he moved around, the glass panes showed his shape and movement as the panes moved. In her dream, it wasn't a jungle. It was set in this hotel. She watched helplessly as the glass monster followed Corwin into Sophie's suite. And came out a few minutes later holding a book in its see-through hand.

Then the scene shifted to the parking lot, where the monster stood absolutely still and invisible against the far wall, until Zac pulled in and parked. The monster waited until no one else was present, then waveringly moved to the van, jerked open the door, and threw Zac to the ground. It then crawled into the van. That's when Jane woke up. Her heart was thumping, her face felt hot and sweaty. She staggered to the bathroom and washed her face in cold water. It took her a full hour to go back to sleep. She wished she'd never seen that movie.

Eighteen

Jane dutifully went to the first session Sunday morning, hoping to learn another aspect of viewpoint. The panelists were different writers this time. Both men. And they said almost exactly what the earlier speakers had said before. Shelley hadn't wanted to come along, so afterward Jane went by herself to a bagel place at the food court in the shopping area, bought a bagel and a glass of green iced tea, and sat there reading a book until ten. Then she went to the house phone. "Could you put me in touch with guest Zac Zebra?"

After a long pause the clerk said, "We don't have anyone registered under that name."

"Oh, I failed to call him by his real name. Harold Spotswood."

"I'll connect you."

In that instant Jane realized she should have rehearsed what to say. She'd have to wing it tactfully. Naturally, he didn't know who in the world she was and probably didn't care. When a man answered, she asked if he was Zac Zebra.

"Yes. Who is this?" He sounded surly. No wonder. He probably still had a headache.

Jane used her nicest voice. "I'm Jane Jeffry. I'm attending this conference and a friend of mine was the first police officer on the scene of your accident."

"Yeah? I'm supposed to thank him?"

"No." *Stay sweet*, she reminded herself. "He told me that you had a page of a book in your hand. I'm concerned that you and Ms. Sophie Smith might still be in danger. Would you have a moment to speak to me privately and see if you can tell me who wrote the page you were holding?"

"I have no idea what the hell you're talking about."

"I think you might when you see it. It might be important to you."

"I don't recognize your name. You aren't a mystery writer, are you? I don't remember reviewing books by a Jane Jeffry."

"I hope you will, when and if I become published," she said to placate him. He could vent his spleen on her much later perhaps. "Please just give me five minutes of your valuable time. I know you probably don't feel well. Could we meet by the elevator lobby on your floor?" Jane felt strongly that she didn't want to go into this man's room on her own. Neither did she wish to drag him clear down to the ground floor.

"Oh, okay, okay," he groaned. "It's the top floor."

"I'll be up in a moment."

Zac wasn't himself. He looked more like she imagined Harold Spotswood would. He wasn't in one of his black-and-white outfits. He wore faded, baggy jeans and an old faded yellow sweatshirt, and was leaning against the far wall, with his hand over his eyes. When he glanced up, his face was so pale she was afraid he was about to faint.

"Please sit down before you fall down," she said, taking his arm to help lower him onto a little bench.

"No. There's a bar at the far end of this hall," he said. "Help me down there. I'm badly in need of a drink."

Jane didn't think this was a good idea, but who was she to argue with her quarry? Oddly enough, it was the same floor she and Shelley were on, and she hadn't known what was at the other end of the floor. She gingerly put one arm around his waist to hold him up. He leaned heavily against her as she led him carefully toward the bar.

The bar was private to the suites. They had to show their room keys. There were only two other customers and they were together at the bar. She hoisted Zac into a very comfortable chair near a good light and said, "Just relax. What do you want to drink?"

"Scotch on the rocks."

She bought his drink, tipped the bartender well, grabbed a bowl of pretzels, then set the drink and pretzels down in front of Zac. She waited patiently until he'd knocked back the first few gulps, then she pulled a copy of the two pages out of her purse.

"Do you recognize these pages?"

"I can hardly see them," he said. "What's this all about, lady?"

Jane stood up and tilted the light to better illuminate the pages. He leaned over and read for a minute or two. "I wrote this. Where the hell did you find it?"

"You had it in your hand when a passerby found you in the parking lot."

He suddenly looked more alert.

"How did you come by it?"

"I'll tell you all about it when you're feeling better. Eat some of these pretzels with your drink."

He slowly read through the pages, then passed the pages back and did as she said. Again, he put his hand over his eyes. But not from pain, she thought. He was remembering something. At least she hoped he was.

"It's coming back," he said. Then he didn't speak for another few minutes. "I gave a copy to Sophie, and Corwin told me she lost it." He paused to munch a couple of pretzels, then said, "It was a book I wrote long ago and I was bringing her another. It was the last one I'd kept. What became of the rest of the book? Do you have any idea what it means to a writer to not have a single copy of the book he worked so hard on? To have it simply not exist anymore?"

"I understand it a little. I once completely lost chapter three of the book I'm working on. I hadn't printed it out and somehow I erased it. I spent a whole day trying to find it. They say nothing is ever completely gone from a computer, but I never found it."

"What did you do?"

"I rewrote it. And it was much better than before. As for your book, it's probably still in your van. The police have the original page. If you want me to call them and tell them to save it, I will."

"Please do. Take my car keys and see if the rest of the book is still in the van, would you?"

"Of course. But only if you eat the whole bowl of pretzels while I'm gone. Where is your van parked?"

"On the north side of the hotel. It's dark blue."

She rose quickly, meaning to take Shelley along. But she was afraid getting Shelley would take too much time. She didn't want Zac to disappear or become thoroughly drunk.

The moment she was out of the elevator, she called Mel and said, "Would you please save that page you faxed me?"

"Janey! What *is* this obsession?"

"I don't have time to explain. Please just take my word that it's important."

There was a long silence before he said, "You're meddling in something that's none of your business and probably dangerous, aren't you?"

"Not in the least. I must go. I'll get back to you later to explain."

She'd been making this promise to too many people in the last few minutes.

The parking lot was deserted and she harked back to Mel's accusation. She hurried to the van, unlocked it, hopped in, and relocked the doors while she hunted. She was still haunted by the dream she'd had last night. She could imagine the glass monster suddenly appearing in the window.

Finally she found the book half under the passenger seat. At least she assumed it was the right book. It had fallen to pieces. She stacked them up the best she could and dumped some newer books out of a plastic bag and put the old book in it.

Looking carefully to see who might be around, and finding the small lot behind the hotel still deserted, and no monster in view, she climbed out of the van, locked it back up, bolted for the front of the hotel, and took the elevator back to the top floor.

Zac was still where she'd left him. His normal color had returned. The bowl of pretzels was empty. He looked more alert and hadn't even finished the drink.

Jane put the plastic bag down on the table, and he all but fell on it. "Where did you find it?"

"Under the front passenger seat."

"Why would I have put it there?" Zac asked himself. "I don't suppose I'll ever remember the reason."

"You don't have to," Jane assured him. "Better that than reliving the whole incident."

"How can I ever thank you enough?"

"Give me a good review without the words 'powder puff' in it, if I ever get published," Jane said with a smile. "Now tell me why putting this book in Sophie's hands was so important."

He did so.

After listening to his explanation, Jane said, "That was first on my list of suspicions. I think you, I, and my friend Shelley should make a point of finding Sophie Smith as quickly as we can. Are you feeling well enough to do that yet?"

Nineteen

"Stay right where you are, Zac," Jane said. "Use my cell phone to call Sophie Smith while I find my friend Shelley."

When she completed the long gallop to the far end of the hall at practically the speed of light, she burst into the room and told Shelley what Zac had told her.

"I know all about it. I've been on the computer. I found Vernetta's e-pubbed book and did a search for an unusual phrase on your copy of the pages. I didn't know the work was Zac's though. She's plagiarized his book and probably plagiarized someone else's as well. I read part of the woman character's scenes and they're an entirely different style. Is Zac with you?"

"No. He's at the other end of the hall."

"Then I can be honest. The other person's work is good. Lots better than Zac's writing. Just as boring a concept, however. How did you figure out it was Zac's work?" Shelley asked.

"I don't have time to explain. I'll tell you all

about it later," Jane replied. "This is the third time I've said that to someone. Zac has my cell phone and is trying to reach Sophie Smith. He's in the bar at the far end of this hallway."

"There's a bar on this floor? I wish I'd known," Shelley said distractedly. She gathered up the pages she'd printed out on the little printer connected to her laptop.

They hurried down the hall. Jane introduced Shelley to Zac and asked him if he'd been able to reach Sophie.

"She's waiting for me. She doesn't know the two of you are coming along too."

"Are you feeling well enough to make it to her room? What's the number?" Shelley asked.

"It's on this floor," Zac said. "And I'm mad enough to run down there."

Corwin, Sophie's toadie, opened the door. "Hello, Zac. And who are you two?" he asked.

"Friends of Zac," Jane said, herding Zac and Shelley into the suite.

"Sophie, your visitors are here," Corwin called to her room.

Sophie emerged, dressed up to the hilt in a cobalt blue dress and matching heels. "What is this all about, Zac? And who are these two women you have with you?"

Zac looked at Jane, going somewhat pale again.

"Ms. Smith, I'm Jane Jeffry. This is my friend Shelley Nowack. We're attending this conference. My friend Mel VanDyne was the police officer who was first on the scene of Zac's attack, and he told me Zac had been found with a page of a book in his hand. I asked for a copy of the page and showed it to Zac. It's from the book he gave you at the front desk when you arrived. A book he wrote under a pseudonym."

"Sit down," Sophie said, pointing to the dining room table. When they were all seated, she looked at Zac fiercely and asked, "Were you the one who stole it back?"

"No. Why would I? Someone else did and we think we know who it was. This is my very last copy and I want it returned before you leave," Zac said, pulling the cover and pages from the bag.

Jane looked at Shelley as Shelley handed over the printout.

"This is the same page, Ms. Smith. I found it on the Internet in Vernetta Strausmann's e-pubbed book. Read both copies."

"What in hell is this about? Why are you three taking up my valuable time?" Sophie nearly shouted.

"Read both my page and the printouts and you'll know," Zac said.

Sophie put the pages side by side, running a finger down each line in turn. She stared at the pages for a long time before looking up. "Who put this on the Internet?"

"Your Golden Pig," Zac said. "Vernetta Strausmann."

Sophie Smith's face was contorted with rage.

"That arrogant woman. That utterly arrogant woman! She plagiarized. Probably the whole thing. Thank God we haven't paid her much yet. After all the publicity, how are we going to bury this, Corwin?"

"Don't tell anyone about this yet. None of you," Corwin said. "Somehow we'll find a way out of it."

"You joke? Why should I keep quiet?" Zac asked. "You can try whatever you want to keep your dirty little secret. I'm not obligated to. And neither are these two good women. I'll bet it's no time at all before they figure out whose book she stole for the woman character's point of view."

Shelley and Jane exchanged a meaningful glance and tried not to smile.

"Corwin, call that horrible fat pig of a woman and tell her to bring herself up here right now," Sophie said.

He did as he was told. "Ms. Smith wants to talk to you immediately. Come back up to the suite now. You remember where it is, don't you?"

When he'd hung up, Sophie said, "All of you stay exactly where you are and keep your traps shut until I've spoken to her."

Vernetta and Gaylord took their time to change their clothes. They were back in the country-western outfits they'd been wearing when they'd arrived at the conference.

Vernetta came into the room with a deafening

yodel and said, "Nice to see ya again, Sophie. What's up?"

She sat down at the end of the table and spotted Jane and Shelley and glared. "What are those two doing here?" she shouted angrily. "I know who they are. The women that slut Felicity says are her friends. And what's Zac doing here?"

Sophie sat and stared at her. "You can't figure it out, can you? Ha! Do you expect we're all too stupid to know what you've done?"

"What I've done? What do you mean?" Vernetta asked, her eyes going little, mean, and piggy.

"You plagiarized Zac's book and someone else's," Sophie barked. "You've been found out."

"Plagrized?" What does that mean?"

"It means stealing someone else's work—their intellectual property, a phrase you obviously don't understand," Sophie said at top volume.

"It's copyright infringement," she went on. "It's illegal. You'll be sued in court and return the money we've given you and not receive any of the rest," Sophie said in a now frigid voice.

"What's more, you're a criminal," Sophie continued, putting the cap on her tirade. "I know how you poisoned me with the chocolates you had sent to me. And you could have killed Zac by attacking him for that book. You'll go to jail for this." Sophie's voice had risen to a shriek. "You've made a fool of me. *Nobody* makes a fool of me. I'll watch every step you ever take when you get out of jail someday."

Vernetta crossed her arms over her heavy breasts and sneered. "You're wrong about all of this. This plagrizing stuff is crap. It was a pair of really old books. I checked on the Internet and both of them were out of print. They didn't belong to anyone anymore. It was okay to use them. And I know Zac didn't write that book. It was some other guy. Somebody named Howard or Harold or some such smarty-pants name."

She slapped her large red hands on the table and went on, "And I didn't do anything to your candy and you bet I paid a bundle for it. I even paid extra to have it gift wrapped. I never stole a book from you. I didn't even know what happened to Zac until word got around the conference. You ain't got a leg to stand on, you old tart."

She stood up, her bosom bouncing violently. "C'mon, Gaylord. We're gettin' ourselves a lawyer right now."

She stormed out, dragging Gaylord in her wake.

Silence reigned. Jane, Shelley, Zac, Corwin, and Sophie looked as if they'd been poleaxed.

It was Jane who spoke first, in a faint voice. "I suspect she was telling her version of the truth."

"God help us all if she is," Shelley said.

Twenty

"*You can't mean that,*" Sophie said. "*It's clearly plagiarism.*"

"Oh, that part is absolutely right. She *is* a plagiarist. She's admitted it even though she doesn't realize it," Jane said. "What I meant is I believe that she didn't steal the copy of Zac's book. She didn't poison your candy. She isn't responsible for the attack on Zac himself. She was much too confident on those points. Didn't you notice the change in her voice and stance? It was obvious. She didn't even grasp the concept of copyright infringement, or that it was important."

Shelley stepped in where Jane left off. "We just assumed that since she's immoral—more accurately, ignorant about copyright law, and terribly vulgar—that she's prone to violence. We all have the proof of plagiarism. We have no proof whatsoever that she did any physical harm to anyone."

"So who did?" Corwin asked.

"Who knows?" Jane asked. "Someone with an

entirely different motive, I have to guess. I have no idea who that would be."

"How can we find out?" Sophie asked.

"I'd guess you could ask more questions of the doctors who treated you, Ms. Smith," Shelley suggested.

"They were all idiots. They hadn't a clue," Sophie said.

"But somebody in the hospital probably took all kinds of samples, and since you recovered so quickly they didn't bother analyzing the samples," Shelley insisted. "I think you should contact the CEO or whoever is the head honcho and learn more answers."

"I've already signed out ages ago. They wouldn't keep the samples for that long."

Jane had been thinking of Zac's welfare more than Sophie's.

"We could theoretically ask the police to survey everyone at the hotel and the conference about that parking lot," Jane said. "When and if they used it. If they noticed Zac's van coming or going."

"The same thing applies," Shelley argued. "Zac recovered. If he'd been murdered—forgive me for suggesting that, Zac—but if it *had* happened, they'd have taken it much more seriously and would have already been knee-deep in an investigation."

Sophie, for once, had waited her turn to speak. "I don't have the time or interest in contacting the hospital. I simply won't eat any edible gift a fan or writer gives me again. I still think Vernetta put something in the chocolates."

"So do I," Corwin said.

"When did she give them to you?" Jane asked. It was worth considering, she supposed.

"When I checked in. Not directly in person though. She had them sent to my suite with a note that they were from her."

"When did you eat one?"

"Oh, a couple of hours later. Quite a bit later, in fact. I'd gone over to that mall to get this dress. After such an early flight, I was tired and hungry and didn't want to wait for room service. They're always so slow."

"How many of them did you eat?" Jane asked.

Sophie looked disconcerted and admitted, "All of them. It was a very little box. Only six Godiva soft centers."

"What did you do with the box?" Shelley asked.

"I threw it away, of course. It's long since gone to the dump."

"So, Sophie is safe," Zac said. "What about me? Who else but Vernetta would want to destroy all of the copies of my books—and nobody say almost anyone who read one, please. I freely admit they were dreck. I'm much better at reviewing than writing my own books."

From what Jane had heard, not only from Felicity but also from other writers, Zac wasn't even a good reviewer. He was careless with his reading and hated any book by a woman. He only temporarily liked her and Shelley because they'd been of use to him.

Zac went on, "Vernetta took the trouble to see if the books she was stealing were out of print. She's not as stupid as she seems. I don't believe for a minute that she didn't know all along that I wrote it. All three of my books were under different pseudonyms, but copyrighted under my real name. She couldn't have plagiarized without owning a copy she'd found in some secondhand bookstore."

"How did you find out about it?" Shelley asked.

Zac said, "A good friend of mine had seen her book on the Internet and thought the title sounded familiar. He sent me an e-mail of the site. I'd never have known about the plagiarism otherwise. I'd forgotten after I was attacked, until she," he said, pointing at Jane, "showed me a page."

"How many other people have you told about this?" Jane asked.

"Nobody but the people in this room, the friend who tipped me off, and the literary attorney. To be frank, the attorney urged me to wait to file a suit until the book was published and Vernetta had lots more money. That's why I've kept my trap shut. So far," he added. It was clearly a threat aimed at Sophie.

"But you haven't," Corwin said. "If that was what you intended, why did you give Sophie that book of yours?"

Zac sighed and looked at Sophie. "We go a long way back together, Sophie and me. We've known each other since we started in the business. We've visited over the years at these conferences and exchanged a lot of gossip. I thought, in spite of my lawyer's advice, that she should at least have a chance at knowing what she was in for. If she didn't bother to read the book, I'd be off the moral hook."

"I guess I should thank you for that, Zac."

Jane didn't think Sophie was even trying to sound sincere.

"When you said the book was missing, I suspected you took it seriously," Zac said. "That's why I went home to retrieve the last copy I'd kept. I'd really like to have it back or at least a Xerox of it."

"I'll make sure you do," Corwin said before Sophie could speak.

"I wonder, too, Ms. Smith," Jane said, "if Vernetta took your threats about the copyright infringement seriously. She seemed to think it was trivial and she was in the clear because the books were out of print."

"She was very cavalier about that, wasn't she?" Sophie admitted. "She'll see that I meant it when our attorneys point out that she has to give back all the money we've already advanced her."

"I imagine she's already spent it on those ridiculous clothes and the architectural drawings of her mansion," Corwin said.

"If Vernetta is an actual threat, won't that make her even more dangerous?" Shelley asked, glancing at Zac as she spoke.

"Not with you two ladies looking after me," Zac said with a slight smile.

"We can't be your bodyguards forever," Jane warned him.

She was realizing this discussion wasn't really going anywhere. She and Shelley had done all they could. She'd irritated Mel to a dangerous extent by snooping and asking favors of him. She hated letting this go. But it wasn't any of their business anymore. It was up to the attorneys now.

She stood up and Shelley followed her lead and rose as well. "We need to go along now and leave it in your hands," Jane said. "Zac, would you like help getting back to your room?"

"No, thanks. I'm feeling a lot better now. I'll stay here awhile. Thanks again."

Twenty-one

Jane and Shelley went down the hallway to their suite. Shelley walked. Jane stomped.

When they were inside, Jane flopped into a chair and said, "If I don't have another RC very soon, I'll go entirely mad and my mother-in-law will finally be allowed to have my children to herself."

Shelley obligingly fixed her one the way she knew Jane liked it—a full can in a big glass with very little ice to dilute it. As she handed it to Jane she asked, "Did you really mean everything you said in Sophie's suite?"

Jane had taken her first big gulp and hiccupped happily. "Thanks, Shelley. Exactly right. Cold and strong enough to take my breath away. As for your question, I suppose I did mean what I said. Maybe. I was just so angry that Sophie, Corwin, and even Zac were talking solely about money and reputations. Corwin doesn't surprise me. He seems such a wimpy toady. But Sophie and Zac both suffered at someone's hands and don't seem to give a fig for their own safety. How stupid can they be?"

"Remarkably stupid. Either one of them could have died from what happened to them," Shelley agreed. "So why are you so much angrier about it than I am? They aren't friends of ours. Neither happens to have died, though I agree that they could have. Why should you care so much?"

"Because I was the one," Jane said, "who was obviously brushed off like a mosquito. Even by Zac. I'd done a lot to help him. I even paid for his drink."

"Forget about them, Jane. It isn't worth working yourself into a fit of nerves over them. Or even over paying for something on behalf of Zac."

"I know you're right," Jane admitted, sipping gratefully on her own drink. "I've paid more than the drink cost for a good hamburger. If you'd been me, though, you'd be just as angry. It's the principle."

"I was thinking the same thing. I mean thinking what you told them about their safety, which appears to be the truth."

"So you believed me?"

"I always believe you. Except when you criticize my driving," Shelley said.

"I don't criticize your driving."

"Not in words, usually. You just sit petrified, shaking, putting your hands over your eyes, and periodically hitting your imaginary brake pedal."

Shelley's driving was the last thing she wanted to think about.

"I really think Vernetta hadn't the faintest idea what plagiarism meant," Jane said. "She couldn't even pronounce it correctly. All she knew was that she thought Sophie was being all het up about nothing. But it scared her when Sophie threatened to withdraw the money she was expecting."

"I agree," Shelley said. "But she couldn't have *not* realized it was looking bad for her. She's probably already spent whatever she's been paid on the architect who produced the plans for her teaching mansion."

"And do you also agree that she at least sounded sincere about having nothing to do with what Sophie and Zac suffered?"

"She did sound sincere," Shelley admitted. "But maybe she has a secret gift for sounding sincere when she isn't. We don't really know her, Jane. We just know enough to dislike her enormously. And after all, who else would have had a motive to put Sophie out of the conference by any means at hand, and injure Zac, to keep them from knowing she was a plagiarist?"

"But that doesn't work, Shelley. Even you must admit she didn't know what it meant. Who else could want to injure or kill both Sophie and Zac? Who else had a reason to hate them enough to possibly murder them?"

"Who knows?" Shelley said, still calm. "Jane,

we've both learned a lot this week about the business of publishing. And this must have to do with publishing, right?"

"It must."

"But we don't know about the other hundred and fifty people at this conference. Just the surface descriptions of the main speakers in the brochure. There could be any number of creeps in this group."

"We know Felicity pretty well," Jane said.

"You're right. I believe she's absolutely innocent of everything. She speaks her mind bluntly. Sometimes too bluntly for her own good."

Jane speculated. "Maybe Chester Griffith or this mysterious Miss Mystery have a long and horrible history with both Sophie and Zac. We had no idea that Zac and Sophie had a friendship. And I still don't believe it. Come to think of it, Zac may have stayed behind to negotiate his own financial settlement with Sophie. Or blackmail her into reprinting his old books."

"What a horrible thought," Shelley said. "But Mr. Griffith and Miss Mystery are both involved heavily in the book business and have probably been around both of them many times. Even your LaLane Jones might have had some serious tiff with them."

"I doubt LaLane had anything to do with it. She only came here, I think, to win the contest," Jane said.

"But she's rather strange, still. Keeping all

those notebooks you told me about and even having a special case to carry them around with her."

"That is a bit strange, I'll admit. We both have obsessions nearly as strange as hers, come to think of it. You're obsessed with the IRS and I'm currently obsessed about my new car. But how was LaLane a threat to Sophie or Zac?"

"She was certainly a threat to Sophie with the records she'd kept and her phenomenal memory. In fact, if she hadn't been here, you'd never have guessed that page you had copied was Zac's work."

"But Shelley, she didn't really know," Jane reminded her. "And I was the one who initiated the question to her about whether it might be Zac's work. If she were the perp, she would have told me it was probably someone other than Zac to cover her tracks."

"I'll buy that," Shelley said after thinking over this convoluted reasoning. "But I still think we don't know nearly enough about at least ninety-eight percent of the people who are here. And I can't quite believe Vernetta and Gaylord are as stupid as they behave."

"Zac said that, too," Jane said. "That Vernetta had the common sense to look up his book to see if it was out of print. Not that it matters. But she thought it did. Maybe I was wrong to say anything about plagiarism and then get my knickers in a twist for speaking up."

They were both quiet and thoughtful for a few

minutes. Then Jane said, "But don't you wish we *did* know for sure?"

"We may never know."

"Don't say so. I want to know. If not now, someday. I invested a lot of mental energy in this and even made Mel seriously annoyed with me about my effort to sort it out."

"It's not your responsibility to sort it out, Jane. Nor are we obligated to keep what we know a secret."

"That's true. Why should we? It might be that the other author who was plagiarized is also here. If word leaked out, she might check out Vernetta's web page and find her own work there. Wouldn't that stir the stew?"

"Wouldn't it make us look gossipy and nasty, though?"

"You have a point. But I did promise LaLane to report on what I found out. I have to keep that promise. Let's go look for her."

They finally found her in the food court in the underground shopping area, eating a turkey sandwich. "May we sit down with you, Ms. Jones?" Jane asked. "This my friend and room-mate. We have something to tell you."

LaLane's face lit up. "Please do."

"It was Zac who wrote that page," Jane said.

Shelley said, "And I'm the one who discovered that Vernetta plagiarized his work."

"Vernetta? Who's that?"

"The big noisy woman who's always wearing a

costume. She e-pubbed a book that Sophie Smith contracted her to publish for real."

"That's horrible. Stealing someone else's work is the most unethical thing a writer can do. And it's illegal."

"We know that."

"But does Sophie Smith know it yet?"

"We made sure she did," Jane said. "And so did Zac after he recognized that the page I showed you was from a book of his."

"I've never liked Zac's writing or his reviews, nor his attitude about women mystery writers, but I feel a little bit sorry for him," LaLane said.

"I don't think you need to be," Shelley said. "Zac knows how to take care of himself." She indicated Jane and said, "She had promised to tell you what we learned, and neither of us wanted to break that promise. That's why we told you this."

"I'm glad you did. I'd have hated never knowing."

"Me, too," Jane said. "And now we'll leave you to finish your lunch. But I wanted to thank you for helping us figure this out."

"Please let me know if you learn any more about this," LaLane said. "And I promise I won't tell anyone."

"We will keep in touch if we learn anything else, but we, too, aren't blabbing it elsewhere," Jane assured her.

As they walked back down the hallway toward

the hotel, Jane said, "I'm glad this worked out this way. Our consciences can be clear."

The thing that none of the three women noticed was the woman at the next table to them, sitting with her back to the threesome, and taking copious notes on every word they'd said.

Twenty-two

"Watching LaLane eat her lunch has made me hungry," Jane said. "Let's follow her example and have an early lunch."

"Good idea. Where?"

"Not in the hotel. That mall across the highway is supposed to have a nice restaurant with a spectacular salad bar. Have you been there yet?" Jane asked.

"No, but I've been told the same thing. It would be good to leave here. But I don't want to walk on that overpass between here and there. Would you mind driving us over there?" Shelley asked.

"Okay, but I think we should both check on what our kids are up to before we leave. I don't like using the cell phone in a restaurant. For some weird reason I feel as if it's like using it in church."

When all their children were accounted for, they set out for lunch.

Jane managed the highway interchange without even getting lost or in the wrong lane and felt very smug. But Shelley wouldn't let her park on the outer fringes of the parking lot this time. "I'm much too hungry to walk half a mile," she told Jane firmly.

The restaurant lived up to its reputation. They ordered one sandwich to share and hit the salad bar, which was every bit as good as they'd heard. You could select between ready-made Caesar salads with croutons and capers instead of anchovies, and butter-lettuce ones with big chunks of blue cheese. Or you could build your own salad on a generous plate with a selection of interesting pastas, flavored rice mixes, veggies cut very fine, eggs, and real crumbled bacon instead of the kind that came out of a bottle. There were a multitude of croutons, nuts of every kind, six salad dressings, and eight kinds of thinly sliced cheeses, including Jane's favorite, Gorgonzola. Cottage cheese, crackers, and other mysterious crunchy things were grouped together.

"I'm sorry we even ordered the sandwich now," Jane said, her plate as full as it could be.

So was Shelley's plate. "I can see that we're going to have to come here often," Shelley said. "You could do this ten times without duplicating what you'd had before."

When they returned to their table, their toasted ham and cheese sandwich was divided neatly between two plates, with parsley artfully adorning the rest of each plate.

"You're not going to eat your parsley in a nice place like this, are you?" Shelley asked.

"I certainly am," Jane replied. "I know it's meant to be decorative, but I love the taste. I'm going to grow a lot of it in my garden this year so I can munch on it anytime I want."

"I've already planted a big pot of basil, the red and green kind," Shelley replied, taking a bite of the sandwich and smiling. "I can bring it in the house or garage if a late freeze threatens."

"What a good idea. I'll buy my parsley and big pot Monday when we're back home. I think I'll try the flat leaf kind, too. I hear it tastes even better. I may purchase enough to chop it up and freeze it in little ice cubes so it lasts through the winter."

They fell to trying to finish their sandwiches and salads, and neither could polish off everything they'd chosen so generously. It was nice to talk about ordinary day-to-day household matters instead of books and plagiarism and advances and viewpoints.

"I'm so glad we came here," Jane said, pushing her plates away and stifling a burp. "Do we really have to go back to the conference? Couldn't we just pack up and hit a garden place?"

"There's always time for garden shopping. But we've paid for this and I'm forcing you to stay to the bitter end. I understand there's a final party that ought to be fun tomorrow morning and a breakfast buffet that ought to be good. Then the out-of-towners can catch a lunch flight home."

"This conference is at least one day too long," Jane said again, as the waiter took away their plates and left the bill. "Shelley, let me pay this bill since it was my idea."

Shelley didn't object for once. "I'm so glad we parked so close. I'm not sure I can even waddle that far."

When they returned to the hotel, the lobby was full of frantically talking conference participants. Shelley spotted Felicity trying to edge away from someone who had her cornered, and they went to the rescue. "Oh, there you are," Shelley said to her. "I was afraid we were late for our appointment with you."

"Just on time," Felicity said, glancing at her watch. "I'm sorry," she said to her captor, "I have to leave now."

Walking quickly and followed by Jane and Shelley, she headed for the elevators. They had one all to themselves. "Come up to the suite and take those high heels off," Shelley said.

"Thanks," Felicity said when they were safely alone.

Shelley started pouring them drinks, this time wine. "What's going on down there in the lobby?" she asked as she handed out the glasses.

"All hell has broken loose, a wildfire of gossip is spreading about Vernetta. They're saying she plagiarized at least half her book from an old one of Zac's."

"It's true," Jane said.

"Vernetta's been stomping around accosting anyone she can find, vehemently denying it."

"What's the costume this time?" Jane asked.

"None. Bulging old jeans and a sweatshirt with the name of a singer who does songs for little kids on the front of the shirt. Is it really true about her?"

"Yes," Shelley said. "But I wonder how it circulated."

"Shelley was the one who discovered it," Jane said.

"How?"

"With a copy of that page that was in Zac's hand when he was found," Shelley said. "I found Vernetta's book on the Internet and did a search for a distinctive phrase from the page."

"So you two started this wildfire?"

"We tried not to," Jane said. "We only told one person who'd helped us. And she promised she wouldn't say anything about it to anyone else. I don't believe she did."

"I'd like to know who did. I'll bet it was that woman I think is Miss Mystery. It's exactly the kind of thing she'd love to pass around."

"But where would she have found the information?" Shelley asked.

"Probably eavesdropping on you," Felicity said. "Where were you when you told the one person?"

Shelley and Jane looked at each other in horror. Jane said, "In the food court in the tunnel."

"Was that woman I pointed out to you there?"

"We didn't even notice who else was there," Shelley said. "I'm afraid we may have stupidly started this. We certainly didn't mean to. Oh, we considered shooting off our mouths about it, but decided it wasn't a nice thing to do. We'd have seemed to be the worst gossips in the world if we did."

Felicity took another sip of her drink and said, "You're really not to blame. It would have come out somehow. Who else knew this?"

Jane ticked off the names. "Vernetta and Gaylord, Sophie Smith, Zac, and Corwin. They were all determined to keep it quiet for stupid reasons of their own. All of them were only thinking about the money and their reputations instead of concentrating on the perp of Sophie's sudden, unexplained illness and the attack on Zac."

"Of course they were," Felicity said. "All but Vernetta and Gaylord are pros in the business. That's their priority, however blind that kind of thinking is. What was Vernetta's reaction when she was told she'd been caught out?"

"Complete denial. She claimed it was from a book she knew to be out of print so she was entitled to use it," Shelley replied.

"That's crazy," Felicity said.

"We know. But she didn't. Still, it proves she's not entirely blockheaded. She apparently believed being out of print for a long time made copying it okay," Shelley explained. "It wasn't entirely convincing."

"But when Sophie accused Vernetta of poisoning the chocolates she had given her and attacking Zac, the denial sounded slightly more sincere," Jane explained.

"Sophie hit her with all that? All at once? Good for the old broad. I guess you two heard it all? Were you convinced she really wasn't responsible for anything but the plagiarism?"

"At first I was," Jane said. "But Shelley steered me out of being that dopey."

"How did this confrontation come to take place?" Felicity asked. "Spill the beans."

Shelley and Jane walked her through the whole thing, and Felicity was delighted to hear the details.

"May I share some of this with my close writing pals? Without using your names, of course. The basic premise of the plagiarizing won't be a secret in the business for long. I give it until Monday to be all anyone talks about in publishing circles. But I'd like to share the news that friends of mine ferreted it out all by themselves."

Twenty-three

After Felicity departed, Jane and Shelley halfheartedly started to pack for the trip home the next day.
Shelley had two pillowcases. One for the clothes
that needed dry cleaning, one for the clothes that
could be laundered at home. Jane stuffed all her
dirty laundry into one pillowcase. They loaded up
their book bags, saving only two books each so
they could choose between which one to read at
bedtime. This would be the last night at the hotel
and they wanted to be ready to make their depar-
ture as early and easily as possible.

When they descended to the lobby, it was as
frantic with gossip as it had been the day when
Sophie collapsed right in front of everyone. And
the rumors were just as wild and varied.

"What does the sign say in the conference registration place?" Shelley asked.

"I'll wait to find out until I unload this disgusting pillowcase and the books in my car," Jane
said. "I suggest you do so, too. We look as if we're
sneaking out on our bill, piece by piece."

"We are. Except that there won't be a bill except for room service and our tip for the maid."

They managed to escape without much notice and returned with only their schedules in their book bags, and their purses.

As they crossed the crowded lobby to see what the sign said, they heard all sorts of weird snips of conversations.

"No, it wasn't Vernetta who plagiarized Zac. It was the other way around," a woman with pieces of her cheap red wig shedding on her shoulders claimed.

"Vernetta is so enthusiastic about being published, I'm certain she wouldn't have taken that risk," a terminally nice older man said.

"It isn't Vernetta, it's someone else and I've forgotten the name," a woman barely out of her teens said, then blushed.

"What does plagiarism mean?" a male voice piped up.

"The same as copyright infringement," an unseen woman replied.

"What's that?" the same male voice asked.

A tall woman wearing a short-skirted black suit said to a small group, "I'm a lawyer and what Vernetta has done is illegal. She'll be in big trouble when this gets around."

Jane whispered to Shelley, as they forged their way through the crowd, "She's nearly the only one who has it right."

Shelley, walking a few paces ahead of Jane,

stopped in her tracks, causing Jane to run into her, and said, "We're not talking to anyone about this."

"No, we certainly aren't. We're acting as if we've never heard it," Jane agreed. "We don't want to blow our cover. Someone else can take the blame for this discovery."

By the time they reached the conference check-in area, the big bulletin board that usually had scraps of papers asking where so-and-so was meeting her, and where was the nearest hairdressing salon, was bare except for a large notice saying, "The rumors about plagiarism are rampant. We hope the participants of this conference can put it aside and not discuss it until all the relevant facts are known. It will make the end of this conference more pleasant for everyone."

Underneath this notice, someone had scrawled in green ink, "And keep you from being sued for slander."

"Another good reason to keep quiet," Jane said under her breath to Shelley.

"What's going on next?" Jane went on to say, fishing out her conference booklet from her book bag. "Let's see. Only two seminars. One is random questions that attendees have forgotten to ask so far. That might be interesting."

"Not very," Shelley said. "If they haven't thought of it yet, it's probably not worth discussing."

"There's another quiz sort of thing," Jane said. "I think I'll go to that one."

"I don't like quizzes. I'm going shopping," Shelley said.

Shelley was a first-class shopper. Jane wasn't. Jane only did so when she had a long enough list of things she really needed to make the trip worthwhile.

"Oh, the next session has something even you would like, Shelley. It's described as 'Let your hair down and fess up about the worst book reviews you've ever read.'"

"Now, that might be fun. And possibly good fodder for letters of complaint," Shelley said with a grin. "I'll meet you in the lobby for that one."

Jane was slightly disappointed by the quiz program. It was too much like one of those she'd seen on television where the moderator makes nasty remarks about contestants who give the wrong answers. Jane felt this trend promoted very bad manners as entertainment and wouldn't even let Katie or Todd watch them. And many of the questions really didn't have anything to do with mystery books.

She stuck it out as long as she could, then wandered back to the lobby. It had pretty much cleared out when the sessions began. She went up to the suite briefly to retrieve one of the two books she'd kept there and went back to the lobby to dip into it while she waited for Shelley to turn up for the next session.

A woman came and took the chair next to her. Jane was already caught up in her book and didn't even look up to see who it was. People with good manners didn't interrupt people who were reading.

But this woman did. Good manners weren't her forte.

"Excuse me, but I don't think we've met. I'm Lucille Weirather."

"I'm glad to meet you," Jane said with barely concealed horror, and pretended to go back to reading. It was the woman Felicity and Shelley had pointed out as the probable Miss Mystery. Jane oozed slightly to the right and turned her name tag over so the woman couldn't read it.

"What is your name?" the woman persisted.

"Why do you want to know?" Jane said, knowing she was sounding like Shelley did when she was approached by a stranger she'd taken a dislike to. Over the years, she'd learned a lot about self-protection from Shelley.

"I overheard you and your friend speaking to Ms. Jones in the food court, and you never called each other by name. I wondered if you could tell me more about the plagiarism."

Jane turned and pointed out the sign at the registration desk. "Have you read that? And I'm afraid you've mistaken me for someone else. I know nothing about it and don't even want to. I don't even know what you mean about a 'food court.' "

The woman stood up and said with a wicked grin, "Sorry to have bothered you, dearie."

Not as sorry as I am, Jane wanted to shout after her.

Jane tried to go back into the book and calm down, but the woman had spoiled it for her. She closed the book and glanced at her watch. Shelley ought to be turning up pretty soon if she meant to attend the next session.

A moment later Shelley appeared, walking noisily on her heels and flopped down angrily in the chair across from her. "I'm so angry. That awful woman that Felicity and I think is Miss Mystery cornered me as I was stopping at the drinking fountain."

"She caught up to you, too?"

"What do you mean? Has she been harassing you as well? What did she ask you?"

"She wanted to know my name and all about the plagiarism thing."

"You didn't tell her either, did you?"

"Of course not. I turned over my tag and told her she'd mistaken me for someone else, and I didn't even know what she meant by food court much less plagiarism and didn't want to know."

"Good for you!" Shelley exclaimed. "Almost word for word what I told her. Except I wasn't wearing my tag in the shopping area."

"She obviously wanted to name the two of us as her source." Jane paused, then exclaimed, "Oh, no! We have to find LaLane and tell her what the woman is doing."

Shelley leaped up as if her chair had exploded. "You're right! Do you know where she is or her room number?"

Jane remembered the room number and they called her from the nearest house phone.

"LaLane," Jane said when she answered, "this is Jane Jeffry." She went on to explain what had happened and begged LaLane not to give Miss Mystery their names. "She claimed her name was Lucille Weirather. That's probably not her real name either. So just don't tell our names to anyone who asks you, if you don't mind."

"My lips are sealed. And I assure you I wasn't the one who let the information out."

"We never doubted that," Jane said.

"We never doubted what?" Shelley asked when Jane hung up.

"That she'd spilled the beans."

"I suspected her briefly," Shelley admitted. "But you convinced me it wasn't her."

Twenty-four

"Who else knows us by name?" Shelley asked.

Jane smiled. "I've introduced myself to several dozen people after taking your advice to mingle. None of them remembered my name. Only Felicity. And she wouldn't tell Miss Mystery."

"No, but she might slip up and tell someone else sent in by Miss Mystery," Shelley warned.

"I guess we should catch up with Felicity. Wonder where she'd be. Want me to call her room?"

Jane didn't have to.

"Do I hear my name being taken in vain?" Felicity said from behind them and sat down in the third chair.

"Not in vain," Jane said. "The woman you think is Miss Mystery has gone after both of us to find out our names so she can blame us for telling the plagiarism story. I turned my name tag over, Shelley wasn't wearing hers, and we refused. You were right that she was eavesdropping. We only wanted to remind you not to tell her either."

"I already told her," Felicity said.

"No!" Shelley and Jane both yelped.

Felicity was smiling. "Shelley, I told her that your name is Enid Potts and Jane's name is Olga Strange. You are cousins who live in a home in Alaska so remote that you don't even have electricity and you light your cabin with oil lamps and heat it with wood. There isn't even a road to the cabin. You flew clear to Chicago on your private plane. You keep it in the nearest town, which is fifty miles away and which you drove to in your matching yellow Humvees."

Jane and Shelley were both laughing so hard they were almost falling out of their chairs.

But Shelley finally pulled herself together well enough to say, "I'd rather have been Olga than Enid. It's more glamorous."

"Did she buy that story?" Jane asked.

"She did," Felicity replied. "But she didn't like it. After today she can't possibly find you to try to pump you again. Obviously you don't have Internet access if you don't have electricity."

Jane pulled out the paper in her plastic tag, turned it over, and wrote in the same style, "Hi, I'm Olga Strange" then reinserted it with the new message facing out.

Still chuckling, Shelley did the same thing.

Shelley said, "I can see why you're such a good writer, Felicity. You have a fabulous imagination to think that story up on the spur of the moment."

Felicity preened. "Making up stories is what I do for a living."

"And you do it very well," Jane said. "On another topic, if I may. Is it worth staying here until the closing ceremonies? I want to go home and work on my book so I can fix it and send it on its way."

"I'm stuck here because I flew in and am flying back, so there's no choice. Besides, I hear it's going to be fun," Felicity said.

"Do you have plans for this evening? We're on our own for dinner, the brochure says," Shelley asked.

"No plans at all," Felicity admitted.

"We found the most wonderful restaurant over in the mall across the street. We'd like to go back," Jane said. "Want to come along?"

"I'd love to escape from here. When shall we go?"

"I think we should go early," Shelley said. "We had an early lunch there, and by the time we left, the place was mobbed. How about five o'clock? Then we could find a good parking place, not wait in line, and do some shopping afterwards."

"No shopping," Jane said firmly.

"I'd love to shop," Felicity said. "But as it is, I'm going to have to break the bank and FedEx home all the books I've bought. I won't have room in my suitcase for anything else. I've already purchased some new clothes as well from one of the shops in the tunnel. I'm going to need a forklift to transport this stuff to the airport."

"We'll meet you here at about ten to five, then. You'll love this restaurant," Shelley promised. "And you'll have the thrill of riding in Jane's brand-new Jeep."

"You have a Jeep, too?" Felicity asked Jane. "I love my big Grand Cherokee but it's an old gas-guzzler. I'm thinking of buying a more efficient one."

"This is the new version," Jane said with all her excitement about it returning in a flash. "It's called a Liberty and is slightly smaller and is supposed to have great gas mileage."

Since Jane and Felicity were clearly going to go on and on about Jeeps, Shelley excused herself. "I'm going up to the suite to call home and see how the kids are doing and if my husband's sister Constanza has figured out the code to our safe. See you two later."

Jane took Felicity out to the parking lot and showed off the Jeep. She even let her drive it around the parking lot and was glad to know Felicity didn't drive anything like Shelley did.

Felicity vowed she was going to buy one just like Jane's when she returned home.

It was a good thing that they'd arrived early for dinner. The restaurant was already filling up when they arrived. "It's Sunday," Shelley said.

Lots of families are shopping in the mall and are eating dinner out before going home."

By agreeing to sit in the smoking section next to the bar at the back of the restaurant, they avoided having to be around a great many badly behaved children. The area was all but deserted.

Jane and Felicity had exhausted the discussions of Jeeps. After the three women looked over the menu, the conversation, which they knew this time was private, reverted to Vernetta and her e-dubbed book.

"Jane and I mildly disagree about what Vernetta said when we met with her, Gaylord, Zac, and Sophie," Shelley said.

"What's the disagreement?" Felicity asked.

Jane said, "It's this—I didn't believe her denial of the plagiarism. She obviously didn't know what was called. She knew she'd done it, although she claimed there was nothing wrong with what she did because the book was out of print. But she was very convincingly angry at being accused of the accidents' that befell Sophie and Zac."

"Zac's experience clearly wasn't an accident," Felicity said. "Why did you mention Sophie along with him?"

Jane replied, "I think somebody poisoned her. But not enough to kill her. I suspect it was in the candies Vernetta had sent to Sophie's suite. I think she added something to them and put the package back together very carefully before she sent them to Sophie's suite."

"Why would she do that?" Shelley asked. "So phie was the open door to her fame and fortune.

"Maybe she was afraid with all these writing folks surrounding Sophie here, someone would tip Sophie off to what she'd done. She probably just wanted to put her out of commission for while until the conference was over," Jane said. "She underestimated Sophie's powers of endur ance."

"That could be true," Shelley admitted. "But why would Vernetta or Gaylord attack Zac?"

"If Sophie realized the book Zac had given he was important and it was missing, she probably asked him to bring her another one. Vernetta could have overheard this, or merely assumed she'd do so."

"That means she had to be the one who knew who wrote the book. Do we know she did?" Fe licity asked.

"Apparently it was written under a pseudonym but Zac always copyrighted in his real name," Jane explained. "And she had to have had an old version of it from a used-book store in order to copy it."

"But how would she have known Sophie knew the book was missing?"

"Because she'd stolen it in the first place," Jane said. Then she stopped dead and said, "Wait There was something said . . ."

"Is this another of your Frederic Remington moments?" Shelley asked.

"I'm afraid so."

They had to stop so Shelley could explain to Fe-
city what this strange remark meant. Jane paid
) attention. She was racking her brains for what
ad fleetingly passed through her mind and in-
antly disappeared.

Twenty-five

ane was determined to put the insight aside. What
did it matter? If Zac and Sophie didn't care what
had happened to them, why was it really any of
her business to convince them otherwise? She'd
heard of both of them in the brochure and the advance bulletins. But that was all. They weren't
friends. They weren't even enemies.

She supposed she considered Vernetta an
enemy. That woman was not a moral person. Then
why should she have any interest in what Vernetta may or may not have done? Except that Jane
felt strongly that plagiarism was a bad thing, if not
actually sinful and criminal. She and Shelley had
done what they could—which was significant—to
prove Vernetta was guilty of it. Now it was time to
let it go.

She had no reason to even think about it anymore.
Whatever happened to any of them was no longer
relevant to her. Her only concern was that she and
Shelley not be publicly named as the women who

had figured it out, and Felicity had taken care of that. At least as far as Miss Mystery knew.

She drove Shelley and Felicity back to the hotel after dinner. The lobby was sparsely populated. According to the conference booklet, there was only one activity going on—a round-table discussion of everybody's favorite mysteries. Felicity wanted to attend just in case someone mentioned her. Jane and Shelley tagged along on the understanding that they'd only stay a little while. When two people had cited Felicity as their favorite mystery writer, they felt they'd done their duty, and headed back to the lobby intending to go back to the suite and maybe order up a dessert from room service later.

They were stopped in their tracks by a scene at the front desk. The Strausmanns were checking out. They had an enormous amount of luggage, even a small trunk that presumably held their costumes. A bellhop was loading everything up to take outside. Vernetta was speaking to a tall, dark, cadaverous older man. Was he her lawyer who'd come to Chicago to escort them home to Kentucky? Or maybe their fundamentalist preacher, saving them from the big-city sinners?

"I'm surprised that they didn't stay to the bitter end," Shelley said. "They must have at least one unused costume to wear to the closing ceremonies and lots of nasty things to say to practically everyone."

"Especially us," Jane replied. "I'm glad they're leaving now. I didn't want to run into them again. I doubt they remembered our names, but they'd have recognized us."

"Oh dear, I hadn't even considered that. We have been saved. Let's go upstairs right now so they don't spot us. I think I need a good hot soaky bath to relax."

When they returned once again to the suite, Jane took off her nice clothes and put on her sweats and sat down in the most comfortable chair to read the book she'd started before the Miss Mystery interrogation started. It was a good book, but she kept tending to nod off from shear weariness. This conference had gone on too long, had too many emotional ups and downs, and all she wanted was to go home.

She was unashamedly napping when Shelley yelped her name a few minutes later. Jane leaped up and ran into Shelley's bedroom. Her friend was sitting at the desk and frowning at the screen of her laptop computer.

"What's wrong? You haven't even changed your clothes. I thought you were taking a bath," Jane said.

"Look at this," Shelley said.

Jane couldn't read the computer screen over Shelley's shoulder. "Print it out so I can see it."

It was from Miss Mystery's web site and said:

BULLETIN : PLAGIARISM DISCOVERED

Dear Readers and Writers, remember when we were all talking about the "E-Pubbed Wonder" who received a huge advance from legendary editor Sophie Smith? Mrs. Vernetta Strausmann, the author of the book, has been revealed as a plagiarist at a mystery convention in Chicago.

The clever sleuths who figured this out are a pair of middle-aged women, Enid Potts and Olga Strange. They claim to be cousins, living in a remote cabin together in Alaska. We all know what this means about them, don't we? Ha ha!

Part of the book was copyright infringed (another phrase for plagiarism) from a book that Zac Zebra, the well-known reviewer, wrote years and years ago.

More on this upheaval when I learn the details. Cousins. Right. Ha ha.

Your reporter, Miss Mystery, giving you all the inside dirt the moment it's dug up.

Jane sat down on Shelley's bed. "This is awful."

"Middle-aged women," Shelley quoted angrily.

"Did you understand it? We're not only middle-aged, we're lesbians," Jane said.

"Is that what she meant? I let myself be caught up in the middle-aged part. Okay, that's it. The woman has to pay for this."

"How are you going to do that?"

"I'll show you," Shelley said, rummaging in her suitcase and coming up with a tiny silver digital camera. "I've been waiting to use this. I've read all the instructions. Miss Mystery hides her identity. She won't be able to do it ever again. I'm going take pictures of her and spread them as far and wide as I can."

Shelley threw the camera into her purse and walked out of the suite.

Jane wished her well. But didn't want to follow her and draw attention to the two of them together.

Shelley was back in an hour. She took a little gadget out of the camera and plugged it into a slot in her computer, hit a couple of keys, and a picture of the woman calling herself Lucille Weirather popped up on the screen. It wasn't an especially good photo. It was dark and murky.

"I didn't want to use the flash and alert her," Shelley said. "I took a lot of shots but this one isn't useful. She's in profile and other people are standing behind her. I don't want that."

One by one, she displayed the rest of the photos on the screen. Of the eight pictures Shelley had taken, only two were acceptable. And one of those had another person in the frame.

"I could fix that by cropping the other woman out, if I had to, but I think I'll just go with the other one. Would you call and ask that copy center if they can use disks to print pictures?"

Jane did what she was told. "They can. They're only open for another hour though. We need to hurry."

Shelley asked the copy shop to print up fifty 4-by-6-inch shots. And she purchased several sheets of sticky labels.

On the way back to the hotel, Jane asked, "Are you really sure you want to do this?"

"It's a public service, Jane. She's a slimy eavesdropper and a vicious gossip. Somebody has to blow her cover and it might as well be us. Or rather Enid and Olga. Now let me print up these labels to put at the bottom of each picture."

The labels said, "This is Miss Mystery. Authors, be careful of what you say in her presence."

"Aren't you skirting close to libel or slander, whichever it is?" Jane asked.

"No. I didn't say anything specific enough. I didn't claim she eavesdrops or says nasty things she overheard."

Shelley gave one sheet of labels to Jane, and they sat sticking the labels to the bottom of each picture. "Give Felicity a call, if you would. I'm sure she'd like a few copies for her writing pals."

"May we drop in on you for a moment?" Jane asked Felicity. "Have you seen Miss Mystery's post about Vernetta and us on her web site?"

"No, but someone mentioned it in the elevator. I meant to look it up but have been too busy trying to pack all these things I've accumulated. Come on down." She gave her room number.

·Jane and Shelley took along a printout of the web page and all the pictures.

"Wow, that's unusually nasty of her," Felicity said when she'd read the printout. "I don't remember her ever going after anyone except authors and the jerks who post their loony notes on her bulletin board section. She had no right to cite you two. Even though Enid and Olga don't exist."

Then she took a look at the pile of pictures. "How did you make her stand still to be photographed?"

Shelley said, "I trailed her for an hour, lurking where she couldn't see me and my tiny camera. I didn't dare use the flash and most of them were murky or had other people in the picture. This was the only good one."

"So what are you doing with so many of these?" Felicity asked.

"I want to put one on the conference bulletin board. It will probably disappear when the people staffing it come back in the morning. The rest . . . well, I thought you might want to share them with your writer friends so everyone will know what she looks like."

"That's a brilliant idea. I'll become a heroine. Let me put my shoes on and we'll go downstairs."

Twenty-six

In the rush to have the pictures done of Miss Mystery, Jane and Shelley didn't fail to enjoy their late-night dessert. They both ordered hot fudge sundaes and regretted this choice all night long. They each got up twice during the night to·take antacids.

"The real cure for this is bland food," Shelley said. "We're supposed to meet Felicity for breakfast. We can enjoy watching what she eats while we stick with very slightly buttered toast."

When they reached the lobby shortly after eight in the morning, the whole place was awash in black-and-white copies of Miss Mystery's picture. The woman claiming to be Lucille Weirather was frantically rushing around the lobby and meeting rooms, trying to find and destroy them. But new ones kept reappearing as if by magic.

Felicity had asked them to meet her at the door of the restaurant and they joined her, laughing like loons.

"How did you do that?" Jane asked.

"I gave out the color copies to several writing friends who had access to copiers. They distributed them everywhere at about six this morning. The one we put on the registration bulletin board has disappeared, as we expected. We've done the entire world of mystery writers an enormous favor. She won't ever again get away with this eavesdropping at conferences. Her cover's been blown."

"We've annoyed the planners," Shelley said with a hint of regret. "But it pays them back for posting a notice telling us which subjects we weren't supposed to talk about."

"They'll recover from it," Felicity said. "Often somebody commits an outrage at these conferences. I once went to one where a woman was carrying around a live chicken. Vernetta's offense was a worse one than ours."

"I'm still wondering about who originally wrote the parts from the woman's viewpoint in Vernetta's book," Jane said. "Writers who are concerned should download the e-pubbed version before it's taken off the Internet."

"Most of us who might have been her victims already did so the minute the story got out," Felicity assured them. "Orla put it on a computer disk and made copies for those of our friends who aren't here. At least it's not something of mine. I couldn't have been that boring, even when I was much younger."

"I envy you your circle of friends," Jane said.

"You have me. And Felicity. We're all you need," Shelley said, patting Jane's arm.

"Shelley's right," Felicity said. "One really good friend who understands is worth ten who don't."

Shifting mental gears back to writing, Felicity went on, "What I really find most unbelievable about this is that Sophie ever bought it. It's really a horrible book. Putting aside all the typos and misspellings, it has virtually nothing to recommend it. The characters are cardboard, always whining to themselves about why they're obsessing about this person in their dreams and doing nothing about it. It's far too long and tedious. There's no sense of time or place. No good phrases that make you think 'I wish I'd written that.'"

"Maybe she never read it?" Jane speculated. She'd learned through the publishing magazine she'd subscribed to that there were lowly first readers who cleared out the worst of the manuscripts that arrived by the hundreds every week at publishing houses.

"I doubt it," Felicity said. "Sophie's really choosy about who she thinks should be paid that kind of money."

"What if someone else, say someone higher up than her, had loved it? One of those Harvard Business School people who've never read good fiction and thought it was 'Literature' with a capital L?" Jane asked.

Felicity thought this over for a moment. "I still doubt it. It is possible, though. Publishing has changed a lot in the last few years with all these conglomerates who made their money selling toilet tissue or safe-deposit boxes. Corporate executives who think publishers are ripe plums to be picked at random to raise their profile as intellectuals. People who are nearly illiterate are making important and catastrophic decisions. It's certainly food for thought."

"If that is what happened, isn't Sophie powerful enough to go after whoever did it to her with hammer and tongs?"

"Probably not, if Felicity's right," Shelley said. "Sophie's exalted position might be in danger as well."

"That's a happy thought," Felicity said with a grin. "She'd never be able to derail any new writer's budding career again."

"There are plenty of new young people coming up to do that, judging by my own experience here at the conference," Jane said. "Two of them totally rejected me without even reading my material. Not that I'm even at the budding stage yet. More like a feeble little seed."

"You can't ever let yourself think that way again," Felicity said fiercely. "Now let's order a nice big breakfast before the waiter throws us out."

Jane and Shelley were still feeling a bit rocky from their chocolate overload the night before and or-

dered unbuttered toast and glasses of watered-
down orange juice.

"You two make me look like a pig," Felicity
said, tucking into a spicy Spanish omelette to
which she'd added hot sauce and lots of pepper.

In spite of her strong resolution to forget all
about Vernetta, Sophie, and Zac, a tiny bell at the
back of Jane's mind kept tinkling, as if saying
"Remember, remember."

Somebody had said something revealing in the
meeting in Sophie's suite. Her subconscious was
sure of it, whether Jane cared or not. She wished
she could muffle the thought and enjoy the last
day of the conference.

Just as they were finishing breakfast, a friend of
Felicity's dropped by their table with a huge wad
of copies of Miss Mystery's picture. "Do any of
you need more of these?"

Felicity introduced her to Jane and Shelley, but
didn't give their names. "No, thanks, Sudie.
There are hundreds of them floating around already, and she can't possibly find all of them."

Sudie said, "Then I'll just follow her and replace what she's picked up."

When she was gone, Felicity said, "She's not
even a writer. She's a fan and means well. She
always goes overboard though. I really need to
finish my packing so I can have everything
waiting at the concierge desk when the final activity is over. May I just leave my bill and tip
and let you pay the waiter and give me a copy

of the bill later on? I'm a fanatic about keeping receipts."

"Of course it's okay," Jane said. "I'll protect it with my life."

When Felicity had gone, Jane asked, "What shall we do until this noon thing?"

"Shopping?" Shelley asked faintly, knowing Jane would object.

"Nope. I'm shopped out. I might make one last trip to the book room if the booksellers haven't already started packing up."

"It's still shopping, isn't it? I'll come along."

Each of them managed to snatch up one last book from a bookseller to take upstairs. Shelley picked one out of a box that had been filled but not yet sealed. As they passed the front desk on the way to the elevator, Sophie was chewing out someone at the front desk about her bill. Corwin was standing with his back to her, pretending he wasn't with her.

Sophie said, "I have the receipt in my purse. Corwin, I left it in the room. Go find it."

Jane glanced at Corwin and was astonished at the look on his face. It was purest example of sheer hatred she'd ever seen.

How interesting, Jane thought, frowning, as Shelley pulled her along to the elevator.

Twenty-seven

The elevators were mobbed with conference participants who were going down to the lobby to check
out. There were also families checking out, deal-
ing with tired, overwrought children, luggage,
shopping bags, and backpacks, all of which had
to be removed before anyone could enter the elevator to go up.

Shelley and Jane found themselves nearly
cheek by jowl with Corwin and the rest of the
people who had waited impatiently. All three of
the conference attendees made a successful effort
not to acknowledge each other.

Jane and Shelley were silent all the way to the
suite. When Shelley closed the door behind her,
she laughed and said, "If looks really could kill,
that look Corwin gave Sophie would have vaporized her into a small pile of ash."

"I didn't realize that you saw that, too. He
really despises her," Jane said. "And no wonder.
Treating a grown man like that. Not even a
'please.' "

"A 'please' would have made it marginally less offensive," Shelley agreed.

"You don't think . . ." Jane began.

Shelley stopped her. "No, we're not thinking about Corwin. We've done all we could or should have done. We've stepped out of this and slammed the door behind us."

"But wouldn't you like to know if Corwin or someone other than Vernetta poisoned the chocolates that made Sophie so sick?"

"If someone else found out and told me, yes. That would be mildly interesting."

"And why she or he attacked Zac?"

"That doesn't seem to matter to Zac. Why should it matter to us? What possible reason would Corwin have for doing that?"

Jane knew from that remark that Shelley hadn't entirely shut the door of her own mind to the events.

"Look, Shelley, we assumed that Corwin probably didn't like this job with Sophie, just because nobody possibly could. I suppose our impression was that he was probably well enough paid to tolerate her while looking for a better job and more congenial boss."

"I never gave Corwin much thought. I guess you're right though. So what?"

"Now that we've seen how he really feels, doesn't that alter your view even a little bit? He could have poisoned Sophie, actually trying to kill her so the dreadful Vernetta would be the obvious suspect. That way he could be free to seek another job in publishing without Sophie sabotaging him. As she would. She has no idea of how much contempt he has for her. We do. And she's mean enough to say anything to ruin his chances if he dared to escape from her."

"I'll accept that reasoning. Marginally. But where does Zac come into it?"

"Maybe he doesn't. These might be entirely unrelated events," Jane claimed, knowing as she spoke she wasn't on firm ground.

"Jane, you know that's absurd. It was all about Zac's book and Vernetta's plagiarizing. Vernetta is responsible for that. Now she's on her way back to her trailer house or wherever they live, and it's someone else's problem to bring her to justice."

"You're right about the book being at the center of it. But there must be some connection we're just not seeing clearly."

Shelley dropped wearily onto a sofa. "We don't have to! All we have to do is go to this last ceremony or game or whatever the closing event is, and then go home and return to our own lives."

Jane sat down across from her. "So you don't care if we ever know the truth?"

"I do care. I just don't want us to be the ones who waste our time and effort hunting it down. Unless the part of your brain that produced Frederic Remington comes up with something new. We put two and two together, you working on

Zac and me working at the computer, and found out that Vernetta had plagiarized Zac, and let the proper people know about it. We've done a good job there."

She went on, "With Felicity's help, we've put that awful Miss Mystery in her place. We don't have to unravel something else that we don't truly need to care about."

Jane was hard-pressed to argue any of these points. Shelley was right. They hadn't truly needed to do any of these things. They'd come here to have a good time and learn interesting information that would be valuable to Jane.

Eventually someone else would have pointed out that the book was plagiarized. Felicity had already half believed she knew who Miss Mystery was and would have described the woman and warned her friends if Shelley hadn't taken that picture of her.

What's more, Jane had annoyed Mel by making him find the page Zac had been holding. Just when their romance was going so well. She didn't dare alienate Shelley as well.

Jane sighed, smiled, and said, "You're absolutely right. Let's forget it and survive the rest of the conference and put it out of our minds. I'm feeling better and a bit hungry. May I raid some of those snacks in the cabinet in the mini-kitchen?"

Shelley hauled herself off the couch and said, "You've come to your senses. Let's see what goodies are in there."

They found lots of good things in the cabinet. Fancy little bags of chips, many tiny bottles of excellent booze, pretzels the shape of stars, itsy-bitsy peanut butter sandwiches. They stayed away from the many chocolates stashed in there, but Jane suggested they each have a bottle of brandy with their snack.

"We don't want to be tiddly for the final event, Jane."

"The bottles hold hardly more than a tablespoon. We can't become drunk on them."

Shelley agreed but said, "We could if we drank all of them." And they sat down at the big table with their snacks, sharing little packets. Both women knew they'd been dangerously close to making each other seriously angry for the first time in their long, satisfying friendship, and put all thoughts of plagiarism, publishing, writing, mingling, and the other participants' problems out of their minds.

Twenty-eight

Before the conference's final activities, Jane called home again for the umpteenth time, this time to ask Katie to keep the washer and dryer free because she had so much clothing to wash when she came home.

"Oh, Mom, can't it wait a while? I'm washing all of Todd's bedding already. He's been eating in his bed and it's full of crumbs. And yes, I've already vacuumed his room, if that's your next question."

Jane was astonished at this display of domesticity, and agreed that her clothing could wait until the next day. "I'll be there before two."

When Shelley and Jane entered the meeting room a little bit late for the closing ceremonies, the first thing Jane noticed was that it was an enormous room. Shelley, who knew a lot about hotels, understood. Jane didn't.

"Isn't this where the small rooms were yesterday? Or wasn't I paying enough attention to know where we are?"

"Those rooms for the seminars *are* this room. Look at the breakdown walls where the former walls have been hidden."

"What a great idea! I'd never have guessed. And look at that food!"

Shelley swiveled around and gawked. The back of the room was lined with draped tables that bore an almost alarming assortment of food: sandwiches, chips, dips, salads, desserts, and drinks.

"We really should have read the brochure!" Shelley exclaimed. "Now we've already ruined our appetites for all this gorgeous stuff."

"I haven't," Jane admitted. "We only snacked. Why are these people dressed so weirdly?"

Studying the crowd, Jane felt as if she were at a Halloween party for grown-ups. A great many of the attendees were in costume. Jane and Shelley stood in the long line for food and glanced around and discovered at least three Arthur Conan Doyles, two of them accompanied by his creation, Sherlock Holmes. The third one was with a group of women who were dressed as grubby little boys—Doyle's Baker Street Irregulars.

There were also at least half a dozen Miss Marples with their knitting, prissy dresses, purses, and frumpy hats. Several men and a few women had attended as Hercule Poirot.

There was a whole flock of 1930s butlers in their black uniforms who were gathered together laughing. A few maids of the same era, some

quite glamorous, were on the fringes of this bois-
terous group, with drinks on plastic trays.

Many of the costumes eluded them. Several
ladies were dressed in floral clothing from the
Golden Era of Mystery, with big floppy hats and
strings of cheap fake pearls. These must have been
minor characters from books featuring deadly
garden parties. One gentleman wore golf trousers
that Jane remembered were called bags and
looked a bit like the huge flapping jeans that
teenage boys wore nowadays. Except that they
were gaitered up at the knees.

Shelley muttered, "You'd have to put a cattle
prod to my temple to force me to dress up like
that."

"I think it's sort of cute. But for myself, I agree.
Hey, Shelley, let's have our pictures taken with
the butlers and maids."

"Heaven forbid!"

"Don't be a spoilsport," Jane said as they finally approached the food tables.

They loaded up on tiny ham sandwiches, chips,
dips, salads, and desserts as if they hadn't eaten
for weeks, then looked for a place to sit. Tables for
eight were scattered through the room. Some
were fully occupied. Most had a few empty spots.
They spotted Felicity, surrounded by fans, and
Jane put down her drink in order to slip Felicity's
lunch bill into her hand. She was blessed with a
grateful smile and a wink.

"We want a table with two places together,

don't we?" Jane asked Shelley as they balanced their full plates and wove their way with caution through the banquet room.

Neither of them was still wearing her tag and most of the others weren't either, so when they found a spot and asked if they could join the strangers, they were welcomed with introductions. Shelley said she was Enid Potts and Jane said she was Olga Strange.

There were two published authors at the table who cheered them and asked them to sign their copies of Miss Mystery's picture for posterity. Obviously they'd checked Miss Mystery's web site this morning.

Shelley said, "We are *not* lesbians, we're neighbors; Enid and Olga aren't our real names; and neither of us has ever been to Alaska."

The authors laughed heartily about how well they'd misled Miss Mystery.

Jane whispered to Shelley, "Aren't you glad we didn't go home earlier? It's fun to pretend to be celebrities. We should grab a few of these pictures if they're still around and sign them to ourselves."

A man lurched by their table. A very tall man, wearing heavy shoes that looked as if they'd been built up somehow to make him taller. Jane glimpsed him in profile as he passed, and saw that he was wearing a Frankenstein mask.

"Who's that?" Jane asked the man sitting next to her.

"Sophie Smith's assistant. Corey or some name like that," he said.

"Corwin," Jane muttered. He was the last person, aside from Sophie Smith, she would have expected to be in costume. He reminded her of the horrifying glass man in her awful dream. Something about the way he moved. She involuntarily shuddered and tried to put away the memory.

"Are you cold?" Shelley asked.

"No. Someone just walked over my grave."

"I wonder where that old phrase comes from?" Shelley said, setting off quite a discussion among the others at the table.

The talk then veered to whether *Frankenstein* was really classed as a mystery. Most thought it was, but one woman claimed it was a twisted love story. The man sitting next to Jane declared it pure horror.

Soon waiters hovered nervously from table to table, asking people if they were finished and clearing plates. Another crew of wait staff was taking away the food that was left on the serving tables, and leaving only the drinks.

At the head table, which had been empty during the meal, half a dozen people started assembling. The room became quiet and a short woman took the podium and fiddled with the microphone, finally forcing it down far enough to be heard.

"I hope all of you have enjoyed this conference as much as we have." She went on to call on all

the committee heads to stand up and be introduced and applauded. Then she introduced herself and the rest of the people at the head table.

"These are our judges in the various categories
of costumes. Now line up in like groups, you
clever impostors," she instructed cheerfully.

While those who were in costumes straggled
into line on the right side of the head table, the
speaker went on, "We have no real rules, understand. It's all personal opinion. In each group of
the same characters, whoever we vote the best
representation will win a twenty-dollar gift certificate to next year's conference. Those who are
in a category by themselves will receive a five-
dollar gift certificate to be redeemed by one of the
wonderful bookstore owners who served us all so
well over the last few days."

The parade began with the butlers walking one
at a time before the judges. Some bowed. Some
said, in fake British accents, "Would master like a
glass of port?" They were all hams.

Next were the maids, then the Poirots, the Miss
Marples, the three Conan Doyles, the Sherlocks,
the whole group of Baker Street Irregulars, and
the assorted miscellaneous imitations who explained whom they represented. Corwin wasn't
anywhere in the lineup, Jane noticed. She glanced
around and saw him at the drinks table pouring a
soft drink, then winding his way to the table
where Sophie sat in solitary splendor. She looked
unusually grumpy.

Twenty-nine

"Let's just sit here for a bit and finish our coffee," Jane said. "The elevators will be mobbed."

She turned slightly to make sure Sophie was doing the same thing. Corwin had tossed his Frankenstein face in the trash and discarded the oversized paper coat he'd worn. He was changing his shoes when Sophie spoke to him harshly. Jane couldn't hear the words. Sophie's expression told her.

As Corwin rose, Jane said, "I've changed my mind. This coffee is cold and icky. Let's go."

Shelley raised an eyebrow and asked, "Why are you so fidgety?"

"I've had another Frederic Remington moment. The little bell that kept dinging in the back of my head finally spit it out. Come on. We want to be on the right elevator."

Shelley sighed and took a last sip of her coffee and followed Jane. As they crossed the lobby briskly, Shelley said, "Tell me what this is about."

"No time. And I don't want to rehearse it."

They forced themselves into a crowded elevator and stepped out on their floor. Jane dawdled, pretending to be searching her purse for the room key. Then she suddenly said, "I found it," holding up the key. Shelley showed her that she'd had her own key in her hand the entire time.

Corwin had stepped into Sophie's suite and propped the door open to carry out his and Sophie's luggage. Jane stopped just before they reached the door and peeked in the room. There was no sign of Corwin. He was probably in the bathroom washing off the smell of the rubber mask. She stepped inside, all but dragging Shelley behind her. Removing the doorstop and quietly closing the door, she gestured at the sofa and whispered, "Let's sit down."

"I don't think this is a good idea," Shelley said in a slightly shaky voice.

"We're in no danger. I have the upper hand," Jane replied.

Corwin returned with his suitcase and was stunned to see them. "What are you two doing here? Get out!"

"You have a choice to make. Let me have my say or I'll follow you down and ask you a few questions in Sophie Smith's presence," Jane said. "Which will it be?"

Corwin slammed down the suitcase on a chair and said, "Then proceed with it. Sophie's waiting for me."

Jane asked in a bland voice, "When we were all

in this room, and Sophie told you to call the Strausmanns and tell them to come up here, you asked them on the phone if they remembered the room number."

"Did I? So what?"

"Had they been here before?"

"Only briefly. The morning Ms. Smith came back from the hospital," he said.

"Shelley, would you go downstairs and ask Ms. Smith if that's true, if you wouldn't mind?"

"No!" Corwin said, turning pale. "Sophie had invited them to come up for a drink after the dessert party, and, of course, Sophie was in the hospital by that time. They caught up with me at the party and begged to come up for a drink anyway. I didn't see any harm in it."

"I understand," Jane said, still in a calm but firm voice. "It was a good way to confront them with the fact that they'd stolen Sophie's copy of Zac's book, right?"

"It never crossed my mind to say that. I have no idea where the book went. Ms. Smith probably just threw it away."

"Shelley, I think that's another thing you might want to ask Ms. Smith."

"No!" Corwin said in an angrier voice than last time. "Get out of here, you nosy bitches." He picked his suitcase back up and headed for Sophie's room to fetch her luggage.

Jane didn't move. She said, barely loud enough for him to hear from the next room, "I'll tell you what really happened. Or I'll follow you down and tell you in front of Sophie Smith if that's what you prefer."

Corwin strolled back into the room, having regained his wits. "What happens next if I agree to listen?"

"Absolutely nothing," Jane said with what she hoped was a cheerful smile. "You'll leave this room with the luggage and cope with what you've done all by yourself. And my guess is that you didn't invite them up after the dessert party. You invited them while Ms. Smith was out shopping that first morning to set up both the poisoned chocolates and the theft of Zac's book."

He thought a moment, then slumped into the sofa opposite them, rubbing his eyes. When he looked up, he said, "I despise Sophie. She treats me like a dog on a leash and won't let go of me."

"We know that," Shelley put in, since it finally seemed to be going well for Jane.

"I received Vernetta's manuscript and it was so awful I couldn't believe it found its way past the first reader," Corwin said. "But something about the early part caught my attention. Way back when I was a lowly copy editor, I'd been forced to edit Zac's book, and a couple of especially bad phrases seemed familiar."

"That's how I found it, too, sort of," Shelley said.

Jane nudged her slightly so as to give her the hint to not interrupt Corwin's train of thought now that he'd decided to confess.

He went on, "I thought it was a way to escape from Sophie without her being able to convince anyone else in the business that I was a horrible employee. That's what she'd have done to me for certain if I'd quit."

Both Jane and Shelley nodded agreement.

"The stroke of luck was that Sophie didn't read it. She said it was too long and she was too busy," Corwin went on. "She glanced through it for about two minutes and suggested I ask the guy who owns the publishing company how he felt about it. She thought he'd be flattered that the great Sophie Smith asked his opinion. And he *was* flattered. Of course, he'd probably never read anything except corporate reports, so he didn't read it either, simply approved the huge advance I'd told Sophie she'd have to pay to gain the publicity to make a bestseller of it."

He stood up and said, "I need a drink of water," then left the room for a moment.

When he returned a moment later, he went on, "I thought I was home free until Zac handed Sophie a copy of his book. As soon as she went to the hospital, I threw it in the trash bin outside the front of the hotel and buried it under some newspapers.

"When Sophie called later and wanted me to bring it over to her at the hospital, I said I couldn't find it, and thought I'd dodged the bullet. Until she told me to tell Zac to find her another copy. God knows why she wanted it. She knows Zac is a terrible writer. I didn't hear, however, what he said to her to convince her she needed to read it."

"So you had to attack Zac when he brought back another copy?" Jane said mildly, even though the very words revolted her.

His face grew very red instantly and he nearly shouted, "I did *not* attack him. I'd seen where he parked his van and knew how far away he lived and waited for him to come back to the same spot, which was in sort of a secret parking area most people didn't know about. As he parked, I walked up to the van, but then suddenly he ducked down and disappeared. This alarmed me, and I jerked open the door. He was apparently leaning way over and holding on to the handle to keep his balance and he fell out of the van."

"Is this really true?" Jane asked.

"I'd swear to it on anything you want me to. That's how it happened. It was a stupid accident. I leaned over him and took his pulse, pushed back his eyelids to see if his pupils were both the same. His breathing was regular. He didn't appear to even be bleeding anywhere."

"So why didn't you call the police and report it?" Jane asked.

"I didn't have my cell phone with me and as I headed in the back door of the hotel to find a phone, a couple came out with their luggage. I stood there for a few seconds while they discovered him. The man immediately pulled out his cell phone and called 911. Call me a coward. I was. I was terrified. But I knew the call had been made and I didn't need to stick around."

As he said this, the phone in the suite rang. He picked it up automatically and all of them could hear Sophie yelling at him to move his slow ass and the luggage down right now or they'd miss their plane.

He hung up without a word and looked at Jane. "So?" he asked.

"Take down the luggage," Jane said. She even opened the door for him and said while he struggled with it, "I hope that you, Sophie, Vernetta, and the stupid owner of the publishing company all receive exactly what you deserve." Then Jane put her hand on his arm and said, "Only one more question. Was it you or Vernetta who poisoned the candy?"

"Me. And it wasn't poison. It was a liquid laxative. I'm a diabetic and I have to give myself shots every day. It was easy. And Sophie enjoyed having a delicate digestive system and talking about it in her usual vulgar way all the time. I didn't expect such a small amount to do any real harm. Just keep her in the bathroom until the conference was over. I had no idea she'd eat them all at one time."

"Have you realized yet that you could have killed both Sophie and Zac and be in jail now for a double murder?"

His face paled, and he said in a shaking voice,

"I've thought of nothing else. I'm horrified by what I nearly did."

Jane removed her hand from his arm. He looked at her and asked, "Are you going to tell anyone else about this?"

"We'll decide that later," Jane said.

She closed the door on him and sat back down on Sophie's sofa, exhausted by the confrontation.

She finally said, "I did well, didn't I?"

"You certainly did. I'm so proud of you. I believed him. Did you?"

"Of course. He's as dull as Zac, and a timid, browbeaten man. He was telling the truth and loving himself for getting it off his chest."

"Are you absolutely certain of this?" Shelley asked.

"I don't care. It's really and truly, cross my heart and hope to die, over as far as I care."

"Then let's go home," Shelley said, opening the door. They walked down the hall to remove the last few of their belongings remaining in the suite and to leave a good tip for the maid. Shelley said, "Make me one promise."

"What is it?" Jane said, looking around one more time for anything she might have left behind.

"Promise you'll let me read what your publishing magazine says in the next issue."

"Just think, Shelley. Probably no one else will ever know what you and I know about this."

Please turn the page for an early look
at the next Jane Jeffry mystery

A MIDSUMMER NIGHT'S SCREAM

by

Jill Churchill

Available in hardcover from William Morrow

"You're not the only one here, Steve," another man said. Jane and Shelley were both startled and whirled around to where the voice had come from. He'd been sitting behind them. This man was about the same age as the director. He radiated good will. He rose from the chair and came around to introduce himself to Jane and Shelley as Jake Stanton.

"But in the play, I'm Edward Weston, the hero's younger brother." He was a bit on the beefy side, but much more attractive than the director. He had a mop of unruly curly brown hair, a charming crooked smile, and good teeth. Jane always noticed people's teeth. Shelley always remembered the color of their eyes. Jane could hardly remember the color of her own eyes.

Steve Imry spoke up," Jake, I'm glad you introduced yourself by your script name. That's what we're going to do from now on. I've instituted this policy before, and it works well. It makes for a more cohesive cast."

Jake smiled before he turned to go to the table, and he winked at Jane and Shelley. It was clearly a joke aimed at the pompous director.

The third person had said nothing. She hadn't even taken her eyes from her script.

Jake sat down across the table from her and said to Jane and Shelley, "The sphinx sitting at the far end of the table is, according to our esteemed director, Angelina Smith. The showgirl tramp my big brother is bringing home to meet the parents."

The young woman finally looked up and spoke. "He means my character is a showgirl tramp. My real name is Joani. With an 'I' at the end.'

She was voluptuous and wore a red, clingy top that looked like the top half of bathing suit specifically designed to show off her impressive cleavage. Her hair was so long, and so glossy that Jane supposed it was a wig. Her make-up was a tad on the garish side.

Joani-with-an-i went back to reading her script and Shelley and Jane exchanged a glance. Each knew what the other was thinking.

Everyone was immediately distracted by the entrance of an elderly couple. They stood posed as if they owned the theater and all those who were present. They were obviously waiting for the proper accolades.

"I'm so looking forward to working with you, Gloria and John," the director gushed. Please make yourselves comfortable. Sit anywhere you'd like. Would either of you like a glass of white wine? I have a bottle chilled."

"Good man," John Bunting croaked. He was looking down Joani's cleavage with a leer.

Jane had seen this couple, Gloria and John Bunting, this morning on the local television station. They both seemed to think they were true stars. The interviewer had obviously never heard of them, and asked them chirpily what movies they'd been in.

"Movies?" Gloria had drawled in a surprisingly deep voice for such a small woman, "Oh, dear, too many to remember. But we started in live theater and have always felt more comfortable with a real audience."

The interviewer asked, to his later regret, what famous plays they'd been in. John rattled off a long, slightly slurred list of productions the interviewer (and Jane) had never heard of.

John, ignoring his wife, staggered around the table to sit next to Joani, obviously hoping she'd eventually move in such a way that he could get a good look at her nipples, and leaned close to her, saying, "You sure are a looker."

Joani got a whiff of his breath, and moved her chair away from him and turned her back to continue reading her script.

"John," Gloria said, "Mind your manners." She tossed one of her many wayward scarves around her throat, to make her point. She went around the table and made John sit in another chair while she sat next to Joani. She slapped down his copy of the script in front of her husband.

Professor Imry said, "I know it's unusual to send scripts out before the first reading session, but we're short on rehearsal time and I wanted the Buntings, in particular, to be prepared. I hope you've all read them and have them pretty well memorized already."

Jane studied Gloria Bunting. She looked better in real life than on television. She was about five foot four, slim but not skinny. She, like most aging actresses, had probably had undergone a good deal of plastic surgery. If so, it didn't show. She had a small thin nose, good cheeks with only a hint of wrinkles. Really good shoulders, which didn't seem to be padding. She must have been a very pretty woman when she was younger and was still attractive.

It wasn't easy to guess her age. She could be anywhere from sixty-five to seventy-five. Her luxuriant white, slightly curly hair looked as if it were her own, not a wig. Her eyes were a clear, perceptive light blue. She moved erectly and easily. No hint of arthritis. Only her hands gave away that she was old. A few age spots. A couple of slightly enlarged knuckles. Jane hoped she'd age as well as Gloria Bunting had.

An extraordinarily good-looking, and well-dressed young man had come in the room while Imry finished speaking. He spotted the elderly pair and went to introduce himself. "I'm Denny Roth," he said patting them on the shoulders patronizingly. "You've probably heard of me. I've been in several independent films. One of them won several awards at Sundance."

Jake was still standing near Jane and Shelley and made a small snorting noise and winked at them again. "As an extra, wasn't it, Denny?"

Denny ignored this and took a seat next to the director. Jake sat down next to Denny and made sure to mention Mrs. Jeffry and Mrs. Nowack. "These are our guests who are going to make sure that we get fed and watered. Be extra nice to them if you know what's good for you."

Steven Imry clearly didn't like someone else making the rules and introductions. He stood in front of the head chair and said, "Starting now, we're going to use your character's names at all times as I said before. I've . . ."

Gloria cut him off. "I'm Ms. Gloria Bunting and don't you forget it, young man."

'Gloria is right," her husband agreed. "That's simply not how it works in a *real* theater, Professor. You might wish to be trendy, but it's not professional."

It seemed as if Imry hadn't recognized that this had offended the actress and her husband, or maybe didn't care. "It's a technique I've used before with great success. It gets everyone into the spirit of the play sooner. You'll address me as Professor Imry. Tonight is simply a first reading. No gestures, no movements. We'll get to those to-morrow. I just want to hear you emote."

There were a few muttered groans, but Jane couldn't tell who they came from. The older actors simply shook their heads 'no.' Shelley muttered almost silently, "emote?"

Jane had also cringed at the use of 'emote.' She smiled at Shelley. The longer they'd been friends, the more they thought alike. Most of the time. But not always. They violently disagreed about how books you owned should be treated.

She put this thought aside as the reading started. Jane was surprised at the different ways each actor read. John Bunting, now designated by the director as Mr. Walter Weston, slurred his words, but seemed to have already memorized the script. That surprised her. But on reflection, it shouldn't have. It was probably how he had earned his living from his youth. He looked a great deal older than his wife. He obviously dyed his thinning hair. He'd run to fat and had the bloodshot eyes and the big red nose of a heavy drinker.

His wife, Gloria, who played Mrs. Edina Weston in the script, was letter perfect and didn't even open the script to follow it. She took on a sort of Katherine Hepburn accent when she was speaking.

Joani-with-an-i, wasn't nearly as well prepared, and had to follow each of her lines with her long-nailed, red-painted forefinger.

Professor Imry was appalled. "You should have had this from memory by now, Angeline. I expect you to have it down by tomorrow's first rehearsal," he warned. "At this stage, you could be replaced."

She nodded sullenly, but her attitude was a bit fearful as well.

Denny Roth, who had the role of Todd Weston, the handsome, wayward son who had brought Angeline home to his family as his betrothed, had the script by memory as well, but read as if he were already bored with it. Apparently changing some of Professor Imry's wording, he was was chastised as well. "Read it as if you mean it, and don't improvise."

"It's not my voice the way you've written it. I sound too old. My character's vocabulary and sentence patterns should be his own, not yours."

Jane had just noticed that there were several extra scripts on the table next to her chair at the back of the room. She took one and handed another to Shelley.

Imry's face turned bright red. "This is *my* script. And I'm the director. You will read it the way it's written, and is being directed."

"I'm not as easily replaced as Joani, you know," Todd said. "You don't seem to know my character as well as you should. Where did I go to high school? My parents' are rich. They'd send me to the best private schools. I'd know better grammar than you've let me use in this script. It's absurd

that the script tells me to say 'Angela and *me* are
getting married.' The correct way is 'Angela and
I are getting married,' and I'd be well enough educated to know it."

Imry pretended he hadn't heard. "Continue.
It's Edward's line next."

Edward, who was really Jake, had it memorized. He played a sort of comic relief younger
brother. Somehow he managed to make Imry's
stiff writing light and almost amusing. Jane
thought of all of them, he might be the best actor
of all of them, except for Ms. Bunting.

The next bit of script was spoken by someone
Jane hadn't even noticed before. He hadn't been
introduced. Glancing at the script, she saw that he
had the role of butler Cecil and his real name was
Bill Denk.

"Madam and Sir, cook says luncheon will be
served in ten minutes." He was a young man, but
spoke in the cracked voice of an elderly retainer.

Jane and Shelley both kept an eye on their
watches. Enduring this wrangling wasn't exactly
fun. "Could we slip out now?" Jane whispered.

"Why not. Nobody needs us here," Shelley admitted.

They went outside, found a bench under a
shady tree, and watched for the catering truck.

Shelley found them a place to sit on a wall in the
shade of a small tree. She gestured at the building
and said, "Paul found out that it had a long and interesting history. At the beginning this was a pricey

neighborhood and this building was a nice theater with live actors before radio and television. Then the neighborhood started going to pot, several patrons were robbed on the way to their carriages, and another nicer theater was built elsewhere.

"Over the years," she went on, "it sat vacant for long periods, then was turned into a movie theater. Was closed again. Then a developer bought it and rented it to a church. The church bought two of the small houses next to it to tear down and make parking places."

"How did Paul learn all this?" Jane asked.

"You can hire people who research old papers and do title searches. Anyway, the older people in the church started moving to Florida, or dying off, and they couldn't make the payments, so it was empty again. For a short while it was used as a soup kitchen. Half the dressing rooms were made into that little kitchen and the room where they're meeting now was where the people ate. Then for a while groups could rent out the kitchen and eating room for craft groups. And the final use was for A.A. meetings in the audience seating area. In one of the intervals urban renewal made the neighborhood a lot better."

"Quite an interesting background," Jane said. "Somebody should save that information and post it somewhere in the building. How did it come into Paul's possession?"

"The old guy who'd owned it forever died. His grandchildren didn't want to be responsible for keeping it up, and were going to demolish it and sell the land," Shelley explained. "Paul, as I told you, bought it, and donated it to the college when he realized he couldn't use it for storing food, because it couldn't be brought up to code. So he had it cleaned up, did a few repairs to the roof and brick work and donated it to the college."

"So he managed to save it. That was good of him."

"I'm sort of sorry I dragged us into this," Shelley admitted. "Let's make a deal here. We're not part of the cast. We can call the actors by their real names, okay?"

Jane sighed with relief. "That was going to be my suggestion, too. I'm not good at remembering names anyway, and especially not two sets of names for the same person. I'm curious as to why these rehearsals aren't done during the day."

"It's because the students are on what's called 'Fast Track Summer,' which means they can do a whole semester's work in seven weeks. But they have to take every class every day. With one hour breaks for studying for exams. That's why they can't get here until six."

"That's an interesting concept. I'm going to ask Mike if his college does that."

"I'm going to hide this script and take it home to read tonight," Shelley said. "So far, I'm not much impressed with it."

"I don't like the director," Jane said, "I think it's unfortunate he's also the writer of the script. Too much ego bundled in one person. It's odd about the casting, don't you think?"

"In what way?" Shelley asked.

"With the proper make-up and clothing, the Weston family will look like they're all related. Imry did make good choices in this case"

"You think so?" Shelley was perplexed. "They don't even have the same colored eyes. Both the Buntings are blue eyed, and son's eyes are brown. That's impossible, I think."

Jane said, "Shelley, we see them close up. The audience won't be nearly as close to the actors as we are. Anyway, I wasn't crazy, I have to admit, about Denny."

"What's wrong with Denny? He was right about his character's background and was dead on about 'Angela and me.' "

"But it was wrong of Denny to tackle him that way in front of all of us. He should have taken Imry aside and told him that his grammar was wrong in private instead of showing off in front of all us.

I think I'm having a heat stroke," Jane stood up and said, sorry that she'd brought up the subject of casting. "We don't have to sit out here in the heat any longer, do we? We've lost our shade. The sun's moved."

"I just dragged you out here to air a few opinions. Since we agree, we can wait inside." She glanced at her watch. "The caterer will be parking the van in the back alley any minute now."